HARRAP'S

A Study in Scarlet

A. Conan Doyle

Pour les notes en marge du texte :

21, rue du Montparnasse
75283 Paris CEDEX 06

HARRAP's® est une marque de Larousse SAS
www.harrap.com

ISBN 978 2 81 870824 8

About the author

Sir Arthur Conan Doyle (1859-1930) was born in Edinburgh and studied medicine at the university there. He had an active career as a doctor and ophthalmologist, including volunteering in Bloemfontein during the Boer War[1] and the First World War. But he also wrote historical works and political pamphlets.

Yet it was for his brilliant creation (*A Study in Scarlet*[2], 1881) of the first scientific detective, Sherlock Holmes, that he achieved great fame[3] – so great that after he killed Holmes off to concentrate on his historical work, he was forced to bring the character[4] back to life in *The Hound of the Baskervilles*.

In later years, Conan Doyle converted to spiritualism and was a friend of the magician Houdini[5]. He died of a heart attack in 1930, at the age of seventy-one.

1. [en Afrique du Sud, 1899-1902]

2. Une étude en rouge

3. connut la célébrité

4. personnage

5. [illusionniste américain]

DIRECTION DE LA PUBLICATION : Carine Girac-Marinier

NOTES EN MARGE : Etienne Leyris

RÉVISION DES NOTES : Marianne Mouchot, Sharareh Maljaei

RELECTURE : F. Le Dantec

INFORMATIQUE ÉDITORIALE ET MISE EN PAGES :
Philippe Cazabet, Marie-Noëlle Tilliette

CONCEPTION GRAPHIQUE : Uli Meindl

FABRICATION : Rebecca Dubois

Mot de l'Éditeur

Vous aimeriez lire en langue originale, mais le vocabulaire, les expressions figurées ou la syntaxe vous arrêtent parfois ?

Cette collection est faite pour vous !

Vous trouverez en effet, en note dans la marge, une traduction de certains mots et expressions qui vous permettra d'avancer facilement dans votre lecture.

Nous n'avons pas cherché à vous donner une traduction littéraire de l'ouvrage et nous nous sommes parfois écartés du sens littéral pour vous fournir le sens qui convient le mieux à l'histoire. Aussi les mots sont-ils traduits dans le contexte du texte original.

Les expressions figées anglaises sont, bien entendu, rendues par une expression équivalente en français.

Les allusions à des réalités culturelles du monde anglo-saxon sont expliquées également dans la marge, pour vous aider à mieux comprendre la trame de l'histoire.

Vous aurez ainsi, en regard du texte original, tout le savoir-faire d'un dictionnaire rien que pour vous et adapté à ce livre !

Notre objectif est de vous mener jusqu'au mot FIN en vous donnant les clés nécessaires à la compréhension du récit.

Laissez-vous gagner par l'angoisse, l'humour et le suspense qui règnent chez les maîtres de la littérature anglo-saxonne.

Lire en VO ? You can indeed!

CHAPTER I

Mr. Sherlock Holmes

IN the year 1878 I took my degree[1] of Doctor of Medicine of the University of London, and proceeded to[2] Netley to go through the course prescribed for surgeons in the army[3]. Having completed[4] my studies there, I was duly[5] attached to the Fifth Northumberland Fusiliers[6] as Assistant Surgeon. The regiment was stationed in India at the time, and before I could join it, the second Afghan war[7] had broken out. On landing at Bombay, I learned that my corps[8] had advanced through the passes[9], and was already deep in the enemy's country. I followed, however, with many other officers who were in the same situation as myself, and succeeded in reaching Candahar in safety, where I found my regiment, and at once entered upon my new duties[10].

The campaign brought honours and promotion to many, but for me it had nothing but misfortune and disaster. I was removed from my brigade and attached to the Berkshires[11], with whom I served at the fatal battle of Maiwand. There I was struck on the shoulder by a Jezail[12] bullet, which shattered[13] the bone and grazed[14] the subclavian artery. I should have fallen into the hands of the murderous Ghazis had it not been for[15] the devotion and courage shown by Murray, my orderly[16], who

1. obtins mon diplôme
2. me rendis à
3. les médecins militaires
4. achevé
5. dûment
6. régiment de fusiliers
7. [1878-1880]
8. corps d'armée
9. franchi les défilés
10. pris mes fonctions
11. [Royal Berkshire Regiment]
12. [fusil djezaïl : principale arme à feu des combattants afghans]
13. brisa
14. frôla
15. sans
16. ordonnance

threw me across a pack-horse[1], and succeeded in bringing me safely to the British lines.

Worn with[2] pain, and weak from the prolonged hardships[3] which I had undergone[4], I was removed, with a great train[5] of wounded sufferers[6], to the base hospital at Peshawar. Here I rallied[7], and had already improved so far as to be able to walk about the wards[8], and even to bask[9] a little upon the verandah, when I was struck down by enteric fever[10], that curse[11] of our Indian possessions. For months my life was despaired of, and when at last I came to myself[12] and became convalescent, I was so weak and emaciated that a medical board[13] determined that not a day should be lost in sending me back to England. I was dispatched, accordingly, in the troopship[14] *Orontes*, and landed a month later on Portsmouth jetty, with my health irretrievably[15] ruined, but with permission from a paternal government to spend the next nine months in attempting to improve it.

I had neither kith nor kin[16] in England, and was therefore[17] as free as air—or as free as an income[18] of eleven shillings and sixpence a day will permit a man to be. Under such circumstances, I naturally gravitated to London, that great cesspool[19] into which all the loungers[20] and idlers[21] of the Empire are irresistibly drained. There I stayed for some time at a private hotel in the Strand, leading a comfortless, meaningless existence, and spending such money as I had[22], considerably more freely than I ought. So alarming did the state of my finances become, that I soon realized that I must either leave the metropolis and rusticate[23] somewhere in the country, or that I must make a complete alteration in my style of living. Choosing the latter

1. cheval de bât
2. Épuisé de
3. épreuves
4. j'avais subies
5. convoi
6. blessés
7. me rétablis
8. dans l'hôpital
9. me chauffer au soleil
10. la typhoïde
11. fléau
12. me rétablis
13. commission
14. transport de troupes
15. irrémédiablement
16. ni famille ni amis
17. donc
18. revenu
19. cloaque
20. fainéants
21. paresseux
22. l'argent dont je disposais
23. me retirer

threw me across a pack-horse[1], and succeeded in bringing me safely to the British lines.

Worn with[2] pain, and weak from the prolonged hardships[3] which I had undergone[4], I was removed, with a great train[5] of wounded sufferers[6], to the base hospital at Peshawar. Here I rallied[7], and had already improved so far as to be able to walk about the wards[8], and even to bask[9] a little upon the verandah, when I was struck down by enteric fever[10], that curse[11] of our Indian possessions. For months my life was despaired of, and when at last I came to myself[12] and became convalescent, I was so weak and emaciated that a medical board[13] determined that not a day should be lost in sending me back to England. I was dispatched, accordingly, in the troopship[14] *Orontes*, and landed a month later on Portsmouth jetty, with my health irretrievably[15] ruined, but with permission from a paternal government to spend the next nine months in attempting to improve it.

I had neither kith nor kin[16] in England, and was therefore[17] as free as air—or as free as an income[18] of eleven shillings and sixpence a day will permit a man to be. Under such circumstances, I naturally gravitated to London, that great cesspool[19] into which all the loungers[20] and idlers[21] of the Empire are irresistibly drained. There I stayed for some time at a private hotel in the Strand, leading a comfortless, meaningless existence, and spending such money as I had[22], considerably more freely than I ought. So alarming did the state of my finances become, that I soon realized that I must either leave the metropolis and rusticate[23] somewhere in the country, or that I must make a complete alteration in my style of living. Choosing the latter

1. cheval de bât
2. Épuisé de
3. épreuves
4. j'avais subies
5. convoi
6. blessés
7. me rétablis
8. dans l'hôpital
9. me chauffer au soleil
10. la typhoïde
11. fléau
12. me rétablis
13. commission
14. transport de troupes
15. irrémédiablement
16. ni famille ni amis
17. donc
18. revenu
19. cloaque
20. fainéants
21. paresseux
22. l'argent dont je disposais
23. me retirer

CHAPTER I

Mr. Sherlock Holmes

IN the year 1878 I took my degree[1] of Doctor of Medicine of the University of London, and proceeded to[2] Netley to go through the course prescribed for surgeons in the army[3]. Having completed[4] my studies there, I was duly[5] attached to the Fifth Northumberland Fusiliers[6] as Assistant Surgeon. The regiment was stationed in India at the time, and before I could join it, the second Afghan war[7] had broken out. On landing at Bombay, I learned that my corps[8] had advanced through the passes[9], and was already deep in the enemy's country. I followed, however, with many other officers who were in the same situation as myself, and succeeded in reaching Candahar in safety, where I found my regiment, and at once entered upon my new duties[10].

The campaign brought honours and promotion to many, but for me it had nothing but misfortune and disaster. I was removed from my brigade and attached to the Berkshires[11], with whom I served at the fatal battle of Maiwand. There I was struck on the shoulder by a Jezail[12] bullet, which shattered[13] the bone and grazed[14] the subclavian artery. I should have fallen into the hands of the murderous Ghazis had it not been for[15] the devotion and courage shown by Murray, my orderly[16], who

1. obtins mon diplôme

2. me rendis à

3. les médecins militaires

4. achevé

5. dûment

6. régiment de fusiliers

7. [1878-1880]

8. corps d'armée

9. franchi les défilés

10. pris mes fonctions

11. [Royal Berkshire Regiment]

12. [fusil djezaïl : principale arme à feu des combattants afghans]

13. brisa

14. frôla

15. sans

16. ordonnance

Coup de pouce pour vous aider à bien comprendre le début de l'histoire...

En tant que médecin militaire en convalescence, je m'attendais à couler des jours tranquilles à Londres. Mais, au fil des jours, j'oubliai ma santé ébranlée, la curiosité piquée par mon colocataire, ce jeune chimiste pour le moins excentrique.

C'est en fait pour rendre hommage à ses talents étonnants que j'ai pris la plume.

Dr Watson

PART I

Being a reprint from the reminiscences[1] of John H. Watson, M.D.[2], late[3] of the Army Medical Department

1. souvenirs
2. docteur en médecine
3. ancien

alternative[1], I began by making up my mind to leave the hotel, and to take up my quarters in some less pretentious and less expensive domicile.

On the very day that[2] I had come to this conclusion, I was standing at the Criterion Bar, when someone tapped me on the shoulder, and turning round I recognized young Stamford, who had been a dresser[3] under me[4] at Barts[5]. The sight of a friendly face in the great wilderness of London is a pleasant thing indeed to a lonely man. In old days Stamford had never been a particular crony of mine[6], but now I hailed him[7] with enthusiasm, and he, in his turn, appeared to be delighted to see me. In the exuberance of my joy, I asked him to lunch with me at the Holborn, and we started off together in a hansom[8].

'Whatever have you been doing with yourself[9], Watson?' he asked in undisguised wonder[10], as we rattled through[11] the crowded London streets. 'You are as thin as a lath[12] and as brown as a nut.'

I gave him a short sketch[13] of my adventures, and had hardly concluded it by the time that we reached our destination.

'Poor devil[14]!' he said, commiseratingly, after he had listened to my misfortunes. 'What are you up to[15] now?'

'Looking for lodgings[16],' I answered. 'Trying to solve the problem as to whether it is possible to get comfortable rooms at a reasonable price.'

'That's a strange thing,' remarked my companion; 'you are the second man today that has used that expression to me.'

'And who was the first?' I asked.

'A fellow who is working at the chemical laboratory up at the hospital. He was bemoaning himself[17]

1. cette dernière solution

2. Le jour précis où

3. assistant-chirurgien

4. sous mes ordres

5. [St Bartholomew's Hospital]

6. un grand ami à moi

7. le saluai

8. fiacre

9. Que diable vous est-il arrivé

10. avec un étonnement non dissimulé

11. parcourions dans un bruit de ferraille

12. maigre comme un coucou

13. aperçu

14. Mon pauvre gars

15. Et qu'est-ce que vous fabriquez

16. Je cherche un logement

17. se plaignait

1. avec qui partager

2. Sacrebleu

3. l'homme qu'il lui faut

4. passionné

5. c'est un type tout à fait réglo

6. de ce à quoi il se destine

7. en connaît un rayon

8. décousues

9. connaissances inhabituelles

10. homme à se livrer facilement

11. l'envie lui en prend

12. supporter

this morning because he could not get someone to go halves with him in[1] some nice rooms which he had found, and which were too much for his purse.'

'By Jove[2]!' I cried, 'if he really wants someone to share the rooms and the expense, I am the very man for him[3]. I should prefer having a partner to being alone.'

Young Stamford looked rather strangely at me over his wine-glass. 'You don't know Sherlock Holmes yet,' he said; 'perhaps you would not care for him as a constant companion.'

'Why, what is there against him?'

'Oh, I didn't say there was anything against him. He is a little queer in his ideas—an enthusiast[4] in some branches of science. As far as I know he is a decent fellow enough[5].'

'A medical student, I suppose?' said I.

'No — I have no idea what he intends to go in for[6]. I believe he is well up[7] in anatomy, and he is a first-class chemist; but, as far as I know, he has never taken out any systematic medical classes. His studies are very desultory[8] and eccentric, but he has amassed a lot of out-of-the way knowledge[9] which would astonish his professors.'

'Did you never ask him what he was going in for?' I asked.

'No; he is not a man that it is easy to draw out[10], though he can be communicative enough when the fancy seizes him[11].'

'I should like to meet him,' I said. 'If I am to lodge with anyone, I should prefer a man of studious and quiet habits. I am not strong enough yet to stand[12] much noise or excitement. I had enough of both in Afghanistan to last me for the remainder[1] of my natural existence. How could I meet this friend of yours?'

'He is sure to be at the laboratory,' returned my companion. 'He either avoids the place for weeks, or else he works there from morning till night. If you like, we will drive round together after luncheon[2].'

'Certainly,' I answered, and the conversation drifted away into other channels[3].

As we made our way to the hospital after leaving the Holborn, Stamford gave me a few more particulars[4] about the gentleman whom I proposed to take as a fellow-lodger.

'You mustn't blame me if you don't get on[5] with him,' he said; 'I know nothing more of him than I have learned from meeting him occasionally in the laboratory. You proposed this arrangement, so you must not hold me responsible.'

'If we don't get on it will be easy to part company,' I answered. 'It seems to me, Stamford,' I added, looking hard at[6] my companion, 'that you have some reason for washing your hands of the matter. Is this fellow's temper so formidable[7], or what is it? Don't be mealy-mouthed about it[8].'

'It is not easy to express the inexpressible,' he answered with a laugh. 'Holmes is a little too scientific for my tastes — it approaches to cold-bloodedness[9]. I could imagine his giving a friend a little pinch[10] of the latest vegetable alkaloid, not out of malevolence[11], you understand, but simply out of a spirit of inquiry[12] in order to have an accurate[13] idea of the effects. To do him justice, I think that he would take it himself[14] with the same readiness[15]. He appears to have a passion for definite and exact knowledge.'

1. le restant
2. déjeuner
3. prit un autre tour
4. renseignements
5. ne vous entendez pas
6. en fixant
7. terrible
8. Parlez sans équivoque
9. cela s'apparente à de l'insensibilité
10. pincée
11. par malveillance
12. par curiosité intellectuelle
13. précise
14. se l'administrerait à lui-même
15. empressement

'Very right too[1].'

'Yes, but it may be pushed to excess. When it comes to[2] beating the subjects[3] in the dissecting-rooms with a stick, it is certainly taking rather a bizarre shape[4].'

'Beating the subjects!'

'Yes, to verify how far[5] bruises[6] may be produced after death. I saw him at it[7] with my own eyes.'

'And yet you say he is not a medical student?'

'No. Heaven knows what the objects of his studies are. But here we are[8], and you must form your own impressions about him.' As he spoke, we turned down a narrow lane[9] and passed through a small side-door, which opened into a wing of the great hospital. It was familiar ground to me[10], and I needed no guiding as we ascended the bleak[11] stone staircase and made our way down the long corridor with its vista of whitewashed[12] wall and dun-coloured[13] doors. Near the further end a low arched[14] passage branched away from it[15] and led to the chemical laboratory.

This was a lofty[16] chamber, lined[17] and littered with[18] countless bottles. Broad, low tables were scattered about, which bristled with[19] retorts[20], test-tubes[21], and little Bunsen lamps, with their blue flickering[22] flames. There was only one student in the room, who was bending over a distant table absorbed in his work. At the sound of our steps he glanced round and sprang to his feet with a cry of pleasure. 'I've found it! I've found it,' he shouted to my companion, running towards us with a test-tube in his hand. 'I have found a re-agent[23] which is precipitated by[24] haemoglobin, and by nothing

1. Et il a bien raison
2. il en vient à
3. [les cadavres]
4. tournure
5. dans quelle mesure
6. les ecchymoses
7. l'ai vu faire
8. nous voilà arrivés
9. ruelle
10. J'étais en terrain de connaissance
11. lugubre
12. blanchi à la chaux
13. gris-brun
14. voûté
15. s'en écartait
16. haute de plafond
17. bordée
18. encombrée de
19. hérissées de
20. cornues
21. de tubes à essai
22. tremblotantes
23. réactif
24. précipite en présence de

else.' Had he discovered a gold mine, greater delight could not have shone upon his features.

'Dr. Watson, Mr. Sherlock Holmes,' said Stamford, introducing us.

'How are you?' he said cordially, gripping my hand with a strength for which I should hardly have given him credit[1]. 'You have been in Afghanistan, I perceive.'

'How on earth[2] did you know that?' I asked in astonishment.

'Never mind,' said he, chuckling to himself[3]. 'The question now is about haemoglobin. No doubt you see the significance of this discovery of mine?'

'It is interesting, chemically, no doubt,' I answered, 'but practically —'

'Why, man[4], it is the most practical[5] medico-legal discovery for years. Don't you see that it gives us an infallible test for blood stains[6]. Come over here now!' He seized me by the coat-sleeve in his eagerness[7], and drew me over to the table at which he had been working. 'Let us have some fresh blood,' he said, digging a long bodkin[8] into his finger, and drawing off[9] the resulting drop of blood in a chemical pipette. 'Now, I add this small quantity of blood to a litre of water. You perceive that the resulting mixture has the appearance of pure water. The proportion of blood cannot be more than one in a million. I have no doubt, however, that we shall be able to obtain the characteristic reaction.' As he spoke, he threw into the vessel[10] a few white crystals, and then added some drops of a transparent fluid. In an instant the contents[11] assumed[12] a dull[13] mahogany[14] colour, and a brownish dust was precipitated to the bottom of the glass jar.

1. dont je ne l'aurais pas cru capable

2. Comment diable

3. avec un petit rire dans sa barbe

4. Mais voyons

5. utile

6. les taches

7. enthousiasme

8. longue et grosse aiguille

9. recueillant

10. récipient

11. contenu

12. prit

13. terne

14. acajou

'Ha! ha!' he cried, clapping his hands, and looking as delighted as a child with a new toy. 'What do you think of that?'

'It seems to be a very delicate test,' I remarked.

'Beautiful! beautiful! The old guaiacum test[1] was very clumsy[2] and uncertain. So is the microscopic examination for blood corpuscles[3]. The latter is valueless if the stains are a few hours old. Now, this appears to act as well whether the blood is old or new. Had this test been invented, there are hundreds of men now walking the earth who would long ago have paid the penalty[4] of their crimes.'

'Indeed!' I murmured.

'Criminal cases[5] are continually hinging upon[6] that one[7] point. A man is suspected of a crime months perhaps after it has been committed. His linen[8] or clothes are examined, and brownish stains discovered upon them. Are they blood stains, or mud stains, or rust[9] stains, or fruit stains, or what are they? That is a question which has puzzled[10] many an expert, and why? Because there was no reliable[11] test. Now we have the Sherlock Holmes' test, and there will no longer be any difficulty.'

His eyes fairly glittered as he spoke, and he put his hand over his heart and bowed[12] as if to some applauding crowd[13] conjured up by[14] his imagination.

'You are to be congratulated,' I remarked, considerably surprised at his enthusiasm.

'There was the case of Von Bischoff at Frankfort last year. He would certainly have been hung had this test been in existence. Then there was Mason of Bradford, and the notorious[15] Muller, and Lefevre of Montpellier, and Samson of New Orleans. I

1. test au gaïac [la résine de gaïac change de couleur]
2. approximatif
3. globules sanguins
4. reçu le châtiment de
5. Les affaires
6. dépendent sans arrêt de
7. seul
8. linge
9. de rouille
10. rendu perplexe
11. fiable
12. salua
13. comme en réponse aux ovations d'une foule
14. issue par magie de
15. tristement célèbre

could name a score[1] of cases in which it would have been decisive.'

'You seem to be a walking calendar[2] of crime,' said Stamford with a laugh. 'You might start a paper[3] on those lines[4]. Call it the 'Police News of the Past."'

'Very interesting reading it might be made, too,' remarked Sherlock Holmes, sticking a small piece of plaster[5] over the prick on his finger[6]. 'I have to be careful,' he continued, turning to me with a smile, 'for I dabble with poisons a good deal[7].' He held out his hand as he spoke, and I noticed that it was all mottled over with[8] similar pieces of plaster, and discoloured with strong acids.

'We came here on business[9],' said Stamford, sitting down on a high three-legged stool, and pushing another one in my direction with his foot. 'My friend here wants to take diggings[10], and as you were complaining that you could get no one to go halves with you, I thought that I had better bring you together[11].'

Sherlock Holmes seemed delighted at the idea of sharing his rooms with me. 'I have my eye on a suite[12] in Baker Street,' he said, 'which would suit us down to the ground[13]. You don't mind the smell of strong tobacco, I hope?'

'I always smoke 'ship's'[14] myself,' I answered.

'That's good enough. I generally have chemicals about[15], and occasionally do experiments. Would that annoy you?'

'By no means[16].'

'Let me see—what are my other shortcomings[17]. I get in the dumps at times[18], and don't open my mouth for days on end[19]. You must not think I am sulky[20] when I do that. Just let me alone, and I'll

1. vingtaine

2. catalogue ambulant

3. lancer une revue

4. là-dessus

5. pansement

6. là où il s'était piqué le doigt

7. car je manipule pas mal de poisons

8. constellée de

9. pour affaires

10. se loger

11. le mieux était de vous mettre en contact

12. un appartement en vue

13. parfaitement

14. [variété de tabac très appréciée des marins]

15. suis toujours entouré de produits chimiques

16. Pas le moins du monde

17. défauts

18. J'ai parfois des périodes d'abattement

19. durant des journées entières

20. fâché

soon be right. What have you to confess now? It's just as well for two fellows to know the worst of one another before they begin to live together.'

1. interrogatoire
2. J'ai un bull-terrier tout jeune
3. désapprouve les disputes
4. indues

I laughed at this cross-examination[1]. 'I keep a bull pup[2],' I said, 'and I object to rows[3] because my nerves are shaken, and I get up at all sorts of ungodly[4] hours, and I am extremely lazy. I have another set of vices when I'm well, but those are the principal ones at present.'

'Do you include violin-playing in your category of rows?' he asked, anxiously.

5. plaisir divin

'It depends on the player,' I answered. 'A well-played violin is a treat for the gods[5] — a badly-played one —'

6. l'affaire entendue
7. vous conviennent

'Oh, that's all right,' he cried, with a merry laugh. 'I think we may consider the thing as settled[6] — that is, if the rooms are agreeable to you[7].'

'When shall we see them?'

'Call for me here at noon tomorrow, and we'll go together and settle everything,' he answered.

'All right — noon exactly,' said I, shaking his hand.

We left him working among his chemicals, and we walked together towards my hotel.

8. Au fait
9. comment diable

'By the way[8],' I asked suddenly, stopping and turning upon Stamford, 'how the deuce[9] did he know that I had come from Afghanistan?'

My companion smiled an enigmatical smile. 'That's just his little peculiarity,' he said. 'A good many people have wanted to know how he finds things out.'

10. intéressant

'Oh! a mystery is it?' I cried, rubbing my hands. 'This is very piquant[10]. I am much obliged to you for bringing us together. 'The proper study of mankind is man[1],' you know.'

'You must study him, then,' Stamford said, as he bade me good-bye. 'You'll find him a knotty problem, though[2]. I'll wager[3] he learns more about you than you about him. Good-bye.'

'Good-bye,' I answered, and strolled on to[4] my hotel, considerably interested in my new acquaintance[5].

1. « L'étude propre de l'humanité, c'est l'homme » [Alexander Pope, *Essai sur l'homme*, 1733]

2. Mais vous trouverez en lui un sujet d'étude très énigmatique

3. Je parie

4. pris le chemin de

5. connaissance

CHAPTER II

The Science of Deduction

WE met next day as he had arranged, and inspected the rooms at No. 221B, Baker Street, of which he had spoken at our meeting. They consisted of a couple of comfortable bedrooms and a single large airy[1] sitting-room, cheerfully furnished, and illuminated by two broad windows. So desirable[2] in every way[3] were the apartments, and so moderate did the terms[4] seem when divided between us, that the bargain[5] was concluded upon the spot[6], and we at once entered into possession. That very evening[7] I moved my things round from the hotel, and on the following morning Sherlock Holmes followed me with several boxes and portmanteaus[8]. For a day or two we were busily employed in unpacking and laying out[9] our property to the best advantage[10]. That done, we gradually began to settle down and to accommodate ourselves[11] to our new surroundings[12].

Holmes was certainly not a difficult man to live with. He was quiet in his ways, and his habits were regular. It was rare for him to be up after ten at night, and he had invariably breakfasted and gone out before I rose in the morning. Sometimes he spent his day at the chemical laboratory, sometimes in the dissecting-rooms, and occasionally in long walks, which appeared to take him into the

1. clair et spacieux
2. engageants
3. à tout point de vue
4. le prix
5. marché
6. sur-le-champ
7. Le soir même,
8. grandes valises
9. ranger
10. du mieux possible
11. nous adapter
12. environnement

lowest portions[1] of the City. Nothing could exceed[2] his energy when the working fit was upon him[3]; but now and again a reaction would seize him, and for days on end he would lie upon the sofa in the sitting-room, hardly uttering[4] a word or moving a muscle from morning to night. On these occasions I have noticed such a dreamy, vacant expression in his eyes, that I might have suspected him of being addicted to the use of some narcotic, had not[5] the temperance and cleanliness[6] of his whole life forbidden such a notion[7].

As the weeks went by, my interest in him and my curiosity as to his aims in life gradually deepened and increased. His very person and appearance were such as to[8] strike the attention of the most casual[9] observer. In height he was rather over six feet, and so excessively lean[10] that he seemed to be considerably taller. His eyes were sharp and piercing, save[11] during those intervals of torpor[12] to which I have alluded; and his thin, hawk-like[13] nose gave his whole expression an air of alertness and decision[14]. His chin, too, had the prominence and squareness which mark[15] the man of determination. His hands were invariably blotted with ink and stained with[16] chemicals, yet he was possessed of[17] extraordinary delicacy of touch, as I frequently had occasion to observe when I watched him manipulating his fragile philosophical[18] instruments.

The reader may set me down as[19] a hopeless busybody[20], when I confess how much this man stimulated my curiosity, and how often I endeavoured[21] to break through[22] the reticence which he showed on all that concerned himself. Before pronouncing judgment, however, be it remembered[23], how objectless was my life, and how little there

1. quartiers les plus sordides
2. surpasser
3. il était dans un accès de travail
4. sans quasiment prononcer
5. si
6. bonne tenue
7. n'avaient pas exclu une telle pensée
8. de nature à
9. le plus inattentif
10. maigre
11. sauf
12. hébétude
13. aquilin
14. vif et décidé
15. saillant, carré, dénotait
16. tachées d'encre et de
17. doté d'une
18. de chimie
19. me taxera peut-être
20. de coupable indiscrétion
21. m'efforçai
22. de percer
23. que l'on se souvienne

was to engage[1] my attention. My health forbade me from venturing out[2] unless the weather was exceptionally genial[3], and I had no friends who would call upon me[4] and break the monotony of my daily existence. Under these circumstances, I eagerly hailed[5] the little mystery which hung around my companion, and spent much of my time in endeavouring to unravel it[6].

He was not studying medicine. He had himself, in reply to a question, confirmed Stamford's opinion upon that point. Neither did he appear to have pursued any course of reading which might fit him for a degree[7] in science or any other recognized portal[8] which would give him an entrance into the learned[9] world. Yet his zeal for certain studies was remarkable, and within eccentric limits his knowledge was so extraordinarily ample and minute[10] that his observations have fairly astounded me. Surely no man would work so hard or attain such precise information unless he had some definite end in view. Desultory readers[11] are seldom remarkable for the exactness of their learning. No man burdens[12] his mind with small matters[13] unless he has some very good reason for doing so.

His ignorance was as remarkable as his knowledge. Of contemporary literature, philosophy and politics he appeared to know next to nothing[14]. Upon my quoting[15] Thomas Carlyle[16], he inquired in the naïvest way who he might be and what he had done. My surprise reached a climax[17], however, when I found incidentally[18] that he was ignorant of the Copernican Theory and of the composition of the Solar System. That any civilized human being in this nineteenth century should not be aware[19] that the earth travelled round the sun

1. capter
2. m'interdisait de sortir
3. clément
4. susceptibles de venir me voir
5. accueillis avec enthousiasme
6. l'éclaircir
7. diplôme
8. porte d'entrée
9. savant
10. précise
11. Le lecteur dilettante
12. n'encombre
13. de broutilles
14. pratiquement rien
15. Un jour que je citais
16. [essayiste et historien écossais, mort en 1881]
17. fut à son comble
18. incidemment
19. ne sache pas

appeared to be to me such an extraordinary fact that I could hardly realize it.

'You appear to be astonished,' he said, smiling at my expression of surprise. 'Now that I do know it I shall do my best to forget it.'

'To forget it!'

'You see,' he explained, 'I consider that a man's brain originally is like a little empty attic[1], and you have to stock it with[2] such furniture as you choose[3]. A fool takes in all the lumber of every sort[4] that he comes across, so that the knowledge which might be useful to him gets crowded out[5], or at best is jumbled up[6] with a lot of other things so that he has a difficulty in laying his hands upon it. Now the skilful[7] workman is very careful indeed as to what he takes into his brain-attic[8]. He will have nothing but the tools which may help him in doing his work, but of these he has a large assortment, and all in the most perfect order. It is a mistake to think that that little room has elastic walls and can distend to any extent. Depend upon it[9] there comes a time when for every addition of knowledge you forget something that you knew before. It is of the highest importance, therefore[10], not to have[11] useless facts elbowing out the[12] useful ones.'

'But the Solar System!' I protested.

'What the deuce is it to me[13]?' he interrupted impatiently; 'you say that we go round the sun. If we went round the moon it would not make a pennyworth of[14] difference to me or to my work.'

I was on the point of asking him what that work might be, but something in his manner showed me that the question would be an unwelcome one. I pondered over[15] our short conversation, however, and endeavoured to draw my deductions from it.

1. grenier
2. y entreposer
3. les meubles de votre choix
4. tout le fatras
5. ne peut rentrer, faute de place
6. entassé
7. avisé
8. grenier cérébral
9. Soyez-en sûr,
10. par conséquent
11. de ne pas laisser
12. bloquer l'entrée des
13. En quoi diable cela me concerne-t-il
14. l'ombre d'une
15. réfléchis à

He said that he would acquire no knowledge which did not bear upon his object[1]. Therefore all the knowledge which he possessed was such as would be useful to him[2]. I enumerated in my own mind all the various points upon which he had shown me that he was exceptionally well-informed. I even took a pencil and jotted them down[3]. I could not help smiling at the document when I had completed it. It ran in this way:

1. aucune connaissance qui serait sans rapport avec son objet d'étude
2. susceptibles de lui être utiles
3. les mis par écrit

Sherlock Holmes — his limits

1. Knowledge of Literature: Nil[4].
2. Philosophy: Nil.
3. Astronomy: Nil.
4. Politics: Feeble.
5. Botany: Variable. Well up in[5] belladonna, opium, and poisons generally. Knows nothing of practical gardening[6].
6. Geology: Practical, but limited. Tells at a glance[7] different soils from each other. After walks[8] has shown me splashes[9] upon his trousers, and told me by their colour and consistence in what part of London he had received them.
7. Chemistry: Profound.
8. Anatomy: Accurate[10], but unsystematic.
9. Sensational Literature[11]: Immense. He appears to know every detail of every horror perpetrated in the century.
10. Plays the violin well.
11. Is an expert singlestick player, boxer, and swordsman[12].
12. Has a good practical knowledge of British law.

4. Aucune
5. Très calé en matière de
6. de concret sur le jardinage
7. Distingue d'un coup d'œil
8. De retour de promenades,
9. des éclaboussures
10. Précise
11. Histoires à sensation
12. Pratique en expert la canne de combat, la boxe et l'escrime

When I had got so far in[1] my list I threw it into the fire in despair. 'If I can only find what the fellow is driving at[2] by reconciling[3] all these accomplishments[4], and discovering a calling[5] which needs them all,' I said to myself, 'I may as well give up the attempt at once.'

I see that I have alluded above to his powers upon the violin[6]. These were very remarkable, but as eccentric as all his other accomplishments. That he could play pieces, and difficult pieces, I knew well, because at my request he had played me some of Mendelssohn's Lieder, and other favourites. When left to himself, however, he would seldom produce any music or attempt any recognized air. Leaning back in his arm-chair of an evening[7], he would close his eyes and scrape carelessly at the fiddle[8] which was thrown across his knee. Sometimes the chords were sonorous and melancholy. Occasionally they were fantastic and cheerful. Clearly they reflected the thoughts which possessed him, but whether the music aided those thoughts, or whether the playing was simply the result of a whim[9] or fancy[10] was more than I could determine. I might have rebelled against these exasperating solos had it not been that he[11] usually terminated them by playing in quick succession a whole series of my favourite airs as a slight compensation for the trial upon my patience[12].

During the first week or so we had no callers[13], and I had begun to think that my companion was as friendless a man as I was myself. Presently[14], however, I found that he had many acquaintances[15], and those in the most different classes of society. There was one little sallow[16] rat-faced, dark-eyed fellow who was introduced to me as

1. Parvenu à ce point de
2. où il veut en venir
3. en conciliant
4. talents
5. métier
6. ses talents de violoniste
7. certains soirs
8. grattait négligemment le violon
9. caprice
10. d'une fantaisie
11. s'il n'avait pas
12. ma patience mise à rude épreuve
13. aucun visiteur
14. Bientôt
15. fréquentait beaucoup de monde
16. cireux

Mr. Lestrade, and who came three or four times in a single week. One morning a young girl called[1], fashionably dressed, and stayed for half an hour or more. The same afternoon brought a grey-headed, seedy[2] visitor, looking like a Jew pedlar[3], who appeared to me to be much excited, and who was closely[4] followed by a slip-shod[5] elderly woman. On another occasion an old white-haired gentleman had an interview with my companion; and on another a railway porter in his velveteen[6] uniform. When any of these nondescript[7] individuals put in an appearance[8], Sherlock Holmes used to beg for the use of the sitting-room, and I would retire to my bedroom. He always apologized to me for putting me to this inconvenience[9]. 'I have to use this room as a place of business,' he said, 'and these people are my clients.' Again I had an opportunity of asking him a point blank question[10], and again my delicacy[11] prevented me from forcing another man to confide in me. I imagined at the time that he had some strong reason for not alluding to it, but he soon dispelled the idea by coming round to[12] the subject of his own accord[13].

It was upon the 4th of March, as I have good reason to remember, that I rose somewhat earlier than usual, and found that Sherlock Holmes had not yet finished his breakfast. The landlady[14] had become so accustomed to my late habits that my place had not been laid[15] nor my coffee prepared. With the unreasonable petulance[16] of mankind I rang the bell and gave a curt intimation[17] that I was ready. Then I picked up a magazine from the table and attempted to while away the time with it[18], while my companion munched silently at[19] his toast. One of

1. se présenta
2. d'apparence douteuse
3. colporteur
4. de près
5. débraillée
6. de velours côtelé
7. indéfinissables
8. faisait son apparition
9. de me déranger de la sorte
10. question sans détour
11. le savoir-vivre
12. en abordant
13. de lui-même
14. logeuse
15. mon couvert n'avait pas été mis
16. irritation
17. fit sèchement savoir
18. m'employai à le feuilleter pour tuer le temps
19. croquait silencieusement

the articles had a pencil mark at the heading[1], and I naturally began to run my eye through it[2].

Its somewhat ambitious title was 'The Book of Life,' and it attempted to show how much an observant man might learn by an accurate and systematic examination of all that came in his way[3]. It struck me as being a remarkable mixture of shrewdness[4] and of absurdity. The reasoning was close[5] and intense[6], but the deductions appeared to me to be far-fetched[7] and exaggerated. The writer claimed[8] by a momentary expression, a twitch[9] of a muscle or a glance of an eye[10], to fathom[11] a man's inmost[12] thoughts. Deceit[13], according to him, was an impossibility in the case of one trained to observation and analysis. His conclusions were as infallible as so many propositions of Euclid. So startling[14] would his results appear to the uninitiated that until they learned the processes by which he had arrived at them they might well consider him as a necromancer[15].

'From a drop of water,' said the writer,

'a logician could infer the possibility of an Atlantic or a Niagara without having seen or heard of one or the other. So all life is a great chain, the nature of which is known whenever we are shown a single link[16] of it. Like all other arts, the Science of Deduction and Analysis is one which can only be acquired by long and patient study nor is life long enough to allow any mortal to attain the highest possible perfection in it. Before turning to those moral and mental aspects of the matter which present the greatest difficulties, let the enquirer begin by mastering[17] more elementary problems. Let him, on meeting a fellow-mortal[18], learn at a

1. Le titre d'un des articles était marqué d'un trait de crayon
2. à le parcourir
3. tout ce qui se présentait à lui
4. discernement
5. serré
6. profond
7. peu vraisemblables
8. prétendait pouvoir
9. la contraction
10. un simple coup d'œil
11. pouvoir sonder
12. les plus secrètes
13. Se laisser tromper
14. étonnants
15. nécromancien
16. maillon
17. que l'investigateur s'efforce d'abord de maîtriser
18. autre mortel

glance to distinguish the history of the man, and the trade[1] or profession to which he belongs[2]. Puerile as such an exercise may seem, it sharpens[3] the faculties of observation, and teaches one where to look and what to look for. By a man's finger nails, by his coat-sleeve, by his boot, by his trouser knees, by the callosities of his forefinger and thumb, by his expression, by his shirt cuffs[4]—by each of these things a man's calling[5] is plainly[6] revealed. That all united[7] should fail[8] to enlighten[9] the competent enquirer in any case is almost inconceivable.'

'What ineffable twaddle[10]!' I cried, slapping the magazine down on the table, 'I never read such rubbish[11] in my life.'

'What is it?' asked Sherlock Holmes.

'Why,[12] this article,' I said, pointing at it with my egg spoon as I sat down to my breakfast. 'I see that you have read it since you have marked it. I don't deny that it is smartly[13] written. It irritates me though. It is evidently the theory of some armchair lounger[14] who evolves[15] all these neat little paradoxes in the seclusion[16] of his own study. It is not practical[17]. I should like to see him clapped down[18] in a third class carriage on the Underground[19], and asked to give the trades of all his fellow-travellers. I would lay a thousand to one against him[20].'

'You would lose your money,' Sherlock Holmes remarked calmly. 'As for the article I wrote it myself.'

'You!'

'Yes, I have a turn[21] both for observation and for deduction. The theories which I have expressed there, and which appear to you to be so chimerical are really extremely practical — so practical that I depend upon them for my bread and cheese[22].'

1. métier
2. qu'il exerce
3. aiguise
4. les manchettes de sa chemise
5. le métier
6. clairement
7. Que toutes ces indications réunies
8. échouent
9. à éclairer
10. incroyable galimatias
11. bêtises
12. Eh bien mais
13. habilement
14. quelque désœuvré en chambre
15. développe
16. intimité
17. réaliste
18. bouclé
19. dans le métro
20. parierais contre lui à mille contre un
21. un certain talent
22. gagner mon pain

'And how?' I asked involuntarily.

'Well, I have a trade of my own. I suppose I am the only one in the world. I'm a consulting detective, if you can understand what that is. Here in London we have lots of Government detectives and lots of private ones. When these fellows are at fault[1] they come to me, and I manage to put them on the right scent[2]. They lay all the evidence[3] before me, and I am generally able, by the help of my knowledge of the history of crime, to set them straight[4]. There is a strong family resemblance about misdeeds[5], and if you have all the details of a thousand at your finger ends, it is odd if you can't unravel[6] the thousand and first[7]. Lestrade is a well-known detective. He got himself into a fog[8] recently over a forgery case[9], and that was what brought him here.'

'And these other people?'

'They are mostly sent on by private inquiry agencies. They are all people who are in trouble[10] about something, and want a little enlightening[11]. I listen to their story, they listen to my comments, and then I pocket my fee[12].'

'But do you mean to say,' I said, 'that without leaving your room you can unravel some knot[13] which other men can make nothing of[14], although they have seen every detail for themselves?'

'Quite so. I have a kind of intuition that way[15]. Now and again a case turns up[16] which is a little more complex. Then I have to bustle about[17] and see things with my own eyes. You see I have a lot of special knowledge which I apply to the problem, and which facilitates matters wonderfully. Those rules of deduction laid down in that article which aroused[18] your scorn[19], are

1. dans l'embarras
2. bonne piste
3. tous les indices
4. de les remettre sur la voie
5. Les méfaits se ressemblent tous
6. élucider
7. le mille et unième
8. s'est empêtré
9. dans une affaire de contrefaçon
10. ont des ennuis
11. clarification
12. empoche mes honoraires
13. imbroglio
14. auquel d'autres ne comprennent rien
15. en la matière
16. se présente
17. me démener
18. a suscité
19. mépris

invaluable to me[1] in practical work. Observation with[2] me is second nature. You appeared to be surprised when I told you, on our first meeting, that you had come from Afghanistan.'

'You were told[3], no doubt.'

'Nothing of the sort. I knew you came from Afghanistan. From long habit[4] the train of thoughts ran[5] so swiftly through my mind, that I arrived at the conclusion without being conscious of intermediate steps[6]. There were such steps, however. The train of reasoning ran[7]: 'Here is a gentleman of a medical type, but with the air of a military man. Clearly an army doctor, then. He has just come from the tropics, for his face is dark, and that is not the natural tint of his skin, for his wrists are fair[8]. He has undergone hardship and sickness, as his haggard[9] face says clearly. His left arm has been injured. He holds it in a stiff and unnatural manner. Where in the tropics could an English army doctor have seen much hardship and got his arm wounded? Clearly in Afghanistan.' The whole train of thought did not occupy a second. I then remarked that you came from Afghanistan, and you were astonished.'

'It is simple enough as you explain it,' I said, smiling. 'You remind me of Edgar Allen Poe's Dupin. I had no idea that such individuals did exist outside of stories.'

Sherlock Holmes rose and lit his pipe. 'No doubt you think that you are complimenting me in comparing me to Dupin,' he observed. 'Now[10], in my opinion, Dupin was a very inferior fellow. That trick of his[11] of breaking in on[12] his friends' thoughts with an apropos remark[13] after a quarter of an hour's silence is really very showy[14] and superfi-

1. me sont très précieuses
2. chez
3. On vous l'aura dit
4. Par la force de l'habitude,
5. les idées se sont succédé
6. étapes
7. Voici l'enchaînement des idées
8. car la peau de ses poignets est plus claire
9. épuisé
10. À vrai dire
11. Cette sale habitude qu'il a
12. d'interrompre
13. remarque incidente
14. pleine d'esbroufe

cial. He had some analytical genius, no doubt; but he was by no means such a[1] phenomenon as Poe appeared to imagine.'

'Have you read Gaboriau[2]'s works?' I asked. 'Does Lecoq come up to[3] your idea of a detective?'

Sherlock Holmes sniffed sardonically. 'Lecoq was a miserable bungler[4],' he said, in an angry voice; 'he had only one thing to recommend him[5], and that was his energy. That book made me positively ill. The question was how to identify an unknown prisoner. I could have done it in twenty-four hours. Lecoq took six months or so. It might be made a text-book[6] for detectives to teach them what to avoid.'

I felt rather indignant at having two characters[7] whom I had admired treated in this cavalier style. I walked over to the window, and stood looking out into the busy street. 'This fellow may be very clever,' I said to myself, 'but he is certainly very conceited[8].'

'There are no crimes and no criminals in these days,' he said, querulously[9]. 'What is the use of having brains in our profession. I know well that I have it in me to make my name famous. No man lives or has ever lived who has brought the same amount of study and of natural talent to the detection of crime which I have done. And what is the result? There is no crime to detect, or, at most, some bungling[10] villainy[11] with a motive[12] so transparent that even a Scotland Yard official can see through it.'

I was still annoyed at his bumptious[13] style of conversation. I thought it best to change the topic[14].

'I wonder what that fellow is looking for?' I asked, pointing to a stalwart, plainly-dressed individual[15]

1. certainement pas le

2. [un des créateurs du roman policier français, mort en 1873]

3. correspond mieux à

4. incapable

5. une qualité à son actif

6. manuel

7. personnages

8. imbu de lui-même

9. avec mauvaise humeur

10. cafouilleuse

11. vilenie

12. mobile

13. prétentieux

14. sujet

15. solide gaillard vêtu très simplement

who was walking slowly down the other side of the street, looking anxiously at the numbers. He had a large blue envelope in his hand, and was evidently the bearer of a message.

'You mean the retired[1] sergeant of Marines,' said Sherlock Holmes.

'Brag and bounce[2]!' thought I to myself. 'He knows that I cannot verify his guess[3].'

The thought had hardly passed through my mind when the man whom we were watching caught sight of the number on our door, and ran rapidly across the roadway. We heard a loud knock, a deep voice below, and heavy steps ascending the stair.

'For Mr. Sherlock Holmes,' he said, stepping into the room and handing my friend the letter.

Here was an opportunity of taking the conceit out of him[4]. He little thought of this when he made that random shot[5]. 'May I ask, my lad,' I said, in the blandest voice[6], 'what your trade may be?'

'Commissionaire, sir,' he said, gruffly[7]. 'Uniform away for repairs[8].'

'And you were[9]?' I asked, with a slightly malicious glance at my companion.

'A sergeant, sir, Royal Marine Light[10] Infantry, sir. No answer? Right, sir.'

He clicked his heels together[11], raised his hand in a salute, and was gone.

1. à la retraite
2. Esbroufe et fanfaronnade
3. corroborer ce qu'il avance
4. lui rabaisser son caquet
5. a dit ça au hasard
6. d'une voix parfaitement neutre
7. d'un ton bourru
8. Mon uniforme est au raccommodage
9. avant, que faisiez-vous
10. légère
11. claqua des talons

CHAPTER III

The Lauriston Gardens Mystery

I CONFESS that I was considerably startled by this fresh[1] proof of the practical nature of my companion's theories. My respect for his powers of analysis increased wondrously[2]. There still remained some lurking suspicion[3] in my mind, however, that the whole thing was a pre-arranged episode, intended to dazzle me[4], though what earthly object he could have[5] in taking me in[6] was past my comprehension[7]. When I looked at him he had finished reading the note, and his eyes had assumed[8] the vacant, lack-lustre expression[9] which showed mental abstraction[10].

'How in the world did you deduce that?' I asked.

'Deduce what?' said he, petulantly[11].

'Why[12], that he was a retired sergeant of Marines.'

'I have no time for trifles[13],' he answered, brusquely; then with a smile, 'Excuse my rudeness[14]. You broke the thread of my thoughts; but perhaps it is as well. So you actually[15] were not able to see that that man was a sergeant of Marines?'

'No, indeed.'

'It was easier to know it than to explain why I knew it. If you were asked to prove that two and two made four, you might find some difficulty, and yet you are quite sure of the fact. Even across the street I could see a great blue anchor tattooed

1. nouvelle
2. considérablement
3. Le soupçon rôdait toujours
4. m'éblouir
5. mais quel pouvait être son but
6. en me mystifiant
7. cela dépassait mon entendement
8. avaient pris
9. l'expression de terne vacuité
10. montrant qu'il songeait à autre chose
11. irrité
12. Eh bien
13. les futilités
14. grossièreté
15. réellement

1. sentait son marin
2. maintien
3. les favoris réglementaires
4. Voilà pour
5. quelque peu conscient de son importance
6. autorité
7. posé
8. à première vue
9. m'écriai-je
10. Rien que de très ordinaire

on the back of the fellow's hand. That smacked of the sea[1]. He had a military carriage[2], however, and regulation side whiskers[3]. There we have[4] the marine. He was a man with some amount of self-importance[5] and a certain air of command[6]. You must have observed the way in which he held his head and swung his cane. A steady[7], respectable, middle-aged man, too, on the face of him[8] — all facts which led me to believe that he had been a sergeant.'

'Wonderful!' I ejaculated[9].

'Commonplace[10],' said Holmes, though I thought from his expression that he was pleased at my evident surprise and admiration. 'I said just now that there were no criminals. It appears that I am wrong — look at this!' He threw me over the note which the commissionaire had brought.

'Why,' I cried, as I cast my eye over it, 'this is terrible!'

11. sortir de l'ordinaire

'It does seem to be a little out of the common[11],' he remarked, calmly. 'Would you mind reading it to me aloud?'

This is the letter which I read to him:

My dear Mr. Sherlock Holmes,

12. en faisant sa ronde
13. clochait
14. dépourvue

There has been a bad business during the night at 3, Lauriston Gardens, off the Brixton Road. Our man on the beat[12] saw a light there about two in the morning, and as the house was an empty one, suspected that something was amiss[13]. He found the door open, and in the front room, which is bare[14] of furniture, discovered the body of a gentleman, well dressed, and having cards in his pocket bearing the name of 'Enoch J. Drebber, Cleveland,

Ohio, U.S.A.' There had been no robbery[1]*, nor is there any evidence*[2] *as to how the man met his death. There are marks of blood in the room, but there is no wound*[3] *upon his person. We are at a loss as to*[4] *how he came into the empty house; indeed, the whole affair is a puzzler*[5]*. If you can come round to the house any time before twelve, you will find me there. I have left everything in statu quo*[6] *until I hear from you. If you are unable to come I shall give you fuller*[7] *details, and would esteem it a great kindness if you would favour me with your opinion.*

Yours faithfully,
TOBIAS GREGSON.

'Gregson is the smartest of the Scotland Yarders[8],' my friend remarked; 'he and Lestrade are the pick of a bad lot[9]. They are both quick and energetic, but conventional — shockingly so[10]. They have their knives into one another[11], too. They are as jealous as a pair of professional beauties. There will be some fun over this case if they are both put upon the scent[12].'

I was amazed at the calm way in which he rippled on[13]. 'Surely there is not a moment to be lost,' I cried, 'shall I go and order you a cab[14]?'

'I'm not sure about whether I shall go. I am the most incurably lazy devil[15] that ever stood in shoe leather[16] — that is, when the fit is on me[17], for I can be spry enough[18] at times.'

'Why, it is just such a chance as you have been longing for[19].'

'My dear fellow, what does it matter[20] to me. Supposing I unravel the whole matter, you may be sure that Gregson, Lestrade, and Co. will pocket

1. vol
2. indice
3. blessure
4. ne comprenons pas
5. mystère
6. en l'état
7. de plus amples
8. meilleur des inspecteurs de Scotland Yard
9. les moins mauvais du lot
10. d'un conformisme choquant
11. ne se veulent pas du bien
12. en chasse
13. par la placidité avec laquelle il discourait
14. fiacre [taxi hippomobile]
15. le plus fieffé flemmard
16. que la terre ait porté
17. enfin, quand cela me prend
18. plein d'entrain
19. précisément l'occasion dont vous rêviez
20. quelle importance

all the credit[1]. That comes of being an unofficial personage.'

'But he begs you[2] to help him.'

'Yes. He knows that I am his superior, and acknowledges it to me[3]; but he would cut his tongue out before he would own it to any third person[4]. However, we may as well go and have a look. I shall work it out on my own hook[5]. I may have a laugh at them[6] if I have nothing else[7]. Come on!'

He hustled on his overcoat[8], and bustled about[9] in a way that showed that an energetic fit[10] had superseded[11] the apathetic one[12].

'Get your hat,' he said.

'You wish me to come?'

'Yes, if you have nothing better to do.' A minute later we were both in a hansom, driving furiously for the Brixton Road.

It was a foggy, cloudy morning, and a dun-coloured veil hung over the house-tops, looking like the reflection of the mud-coloured streets beneath. My companion was in the best of spirits[13], and prattled away about[14] Cremona fiddles, and the difference between a Stradivarius and an Amati. As for myself, I was silent, for the dull weather and the melancholy business[15] upon which we were engaged, depressed my spirits[16].

'You don't seem to give much thought to the matter in hand[17],' I said at last, interrupting Holmes' musical disquisition[18].

'No data yet[19],' he answered. 'It is a capital mistake to theorize before you have all the evidence. It biases[20] the judgment.'

'You will have your data soon,' I remarked, pointing with my finger; 'this is the Brixton Road, and that is the house, if I am not very much mistaken.'

1. s'en attribueront tout le mérite
2. vous implore
3. le reconnaît devant moi
4. de le concéder devant un tiers
5. J'éluciderai l'affaire tout seul
6. à leurs dépens,
7. ce sera toujours ça
8. enfila son pardessus à la hâte
9. s'activa
10. phase dynamique
11. remplacé
12. la phase apathique
13. de belle humeur
14. discourait sur
15. triste affaire
16. me mettait d'humeur chagrine
17. en cours
18. dissertation
19. Aucun élément pour le moment
20. Cela fausse

'So it is. Stop, driver, stop!' We were still a hundred yards or so from it, but he insisted upon our alighting[1], and we finished our journey[2] upon foot.

Number 3, Lauriston Gardens, wore an ill-omened and minatory look[3]. It was one of four which stood back some little way[4] from the street, two being occupied and two empty. The latter looked out with three tiers[5] of vacant[6] melancholy windows, which were blank and dreary[7], save that here and there a 'To Let' card[8] had developed like a cataract[9] upon the bleared panes[10]. A small garden sprinkled over with a scattered eruption of sickly plants[11] separated each of these houses from the street, and was traversed by a narrow pathway, yellowish in colour, and consisting apparently of a mixture of clay[12] and of gravel[13]. The whole place was very sloppy from[14] the rain which had fallen through the night. The garden was bounded by a three-foot brick wall with a fringe[15] of wood rails upon the top, and against this wall was leaning a stalwart[16] police constable[17], surrounded by a small knot of loafers[18], who craned their necks[19] and strained their[20] eyes in the vain hope of catching some glimpse of[21] the proceedings within[22].

I had imagined that Sherlock Holmes would at once have hurried into the house and plunged into a study of the mystery. Nothing appeared to be further from his intention. With an air of nonchalance which, under the circumstances, seemed to me to border upon[23] affectation, he lounged up and down the[24] pavement, and gazed vacantly[25] at the ground, the sky, the opposite houses and the line of railings. Having finished his scrutiny, he proceeded slowly down the path, or rather down the fringe of grass which flanked the path, keeping

1. pour que nous descendions de voiture
2. trajet
3. ne disait rien qui vaille
4. s'élevaient un peu en retrait
5. niveaux
6. inoccupées
7. vides et tristes
8. panneau *À louer*
9. proliféré
10. vitres brouillées
11. parsemé d'une série de plantes chétives
12. argile
13. gravier
14. détrempé par
15. bordure
16. robuste
17. agent de police
18. badauds
19. tendaient le cou
20. écarquillaient les
21. apercevoir
22. ce qui se passait à l'intérieur
23. confiner à
24. déambula lentement le long du
25. d'un air absent

his eyes riveted[1] upon the ground. Twice he stopped, and once I saw him smile, and heard him utter[2] an exclamation of satisfaction. There were many marks of footsteps upon the wet clayey[3] soil, but since the police had been coming and going over it, I was unable to see how my companion could hope to learn anything from it. Still I had had such extraordinary evidence[4] of the quickness[5] of his perceptive faculties, that I had no doubt that he could see a great deal which was hidden from me.

At the door of the house we were met by a tall, white-faced, flaxen-haired[6] man, with a notebook in his hand, who rushed forward and wrung[7] my companion's hand with effusion. 'It is indeed kind of you to come,' he said, 'I have had everything left untouched[8].'

'Except that!' my friend answered, pointing at the pathway. 'If a herd[9] of buffaloes had passed along there could not be a greater mess. No doubt, however, you had drawn your own conclusions, Gregson, before you permitted this.'

'I have had so much to do inside the house,' the detective said evasively. 'My colleague, Mr. Lestrade, is here. I had relied upon him to look after this[10].'

Holmes glanced at me and raised his eyebrows sardonically. 'With two such men as[11] yourself and Lestrade upon the ground, there will not be much for a third party to find out[12],' he said.

Gregson rubbed his hands in a self-satisfied way. 'I think we have done all that can be done,' he answered; 'it's a queer case though, and I knew your taste for such things.'

'You did not come here in a cab?' asked Sherlock Holmes.

1. rivés
2. pousser
3. argileux
4. preuve
5. acuité
6. aux cheveux filasse
7. serra
8. veillé à ce qu'on ne touche à rien
9. troupeau
10. comptais sur lui pour qu'il s'en occupe
11. hommes tels que
12. un troisième n'aura plus grand-chose à découvrir

'No, sir.'

'Nor Lestrade?'

'No, sir.'

'Then let us go and look at the room.' With which inconsequent[1] remark he strode on[2] into the house, followed by Gregson, whose features expressed his astonishment.

A short passage, bare planked and dusty[3], led to the kitchen and offices[4]. Two doors opened out of it to the left and to the right. One of these had obviously been closed for many weeks. The other belonged to the dining-room, which was the apartment in which the mysterious affair had occurred. Holmes walked in, and I followed him with that subdued feeling[5] at my heart which the presence of death inspires.

It was a large square room, looking all the larger[6] from the absence of all furniture[7]. A vulgar flaring[8] paper adorned[9] the walls, but it was blotched in places[10] with mildew[11], and here and there great strips had become detached and hung down, exposing the yellow plaster beneath. Opposite the door was a showy[12] fireplace, surmounted by a mantelpiece[13] of imitation white marble. On one corner of this was stuck the stump[14] of a red wax candle. The solitary[15] window was so dirty that the light was hazy and uncertain, giving a dull grey tinge to everything, which was intensified by the thick layer of dust which coated the whole apartment.

All these details I observed afterwards. At present my attention was centred upon the single, grim[16], motionless figure[17] which lay stretched upon the boards[18], with vacant sightless eyes staring up at the discoloured ceiling. It was that of a man

1. déconcertante
2. pénétra à grandes enjambées
3. au plancher nu et poussiéreux
4. à l'office
5. tristesse
6. qui paraissait d'autant plus grande
7. qu'elle était dépourvue de meubles
8. rutilant
9. ornait
10. taché par endroits
11. de moisissure
12. tape-à-l'œil
13. tablette
14. les restes
15. unique
16. macabre
17. silhouette
18. plancher

about forty-three or forty-four years of age, middle-sized, broad-shouldered, with crisp curling[1] black hair, and a short stubbly[2] beard. He was dressed in a heavy broadcloth[3] frock coat[4] and waistcoat[5], with light-coloured trousers, and immaculate collar and cuffs[6]. A top hat[7], well brushed and trim[8], was placed upon the floor beside him. His hands were clenched[9] and his arms thrown abroad[10], while his lower limbs[11] were interlocked[12] as though his death struggle[13] had been a grievous one[14]. On his rigid face there stood an expression of horror, and as it seemed to me, of hatred[15], such as I have never seen upon human features. This malignant[16] and terrible contortion[17], combined with the low forehead, blunt[18] nose, and prognathous jaw gave the dead man a singularly simious and ape-like[19] appearance, which was increased by his writhing[20], unnatural posture. I have seen death in many forms, but never has it appeared to me in a more fearsome[21] aspect than in that dark grimy[22] apartment, which looked out upon[23] one of the main arteries of suburban London.

Lestrade, lean and ferret-like as ever[24], was standing by the doorway, and greeted my companion and myself.

'This case will make a stir[25], sir,' he remarked. 'It beats anything I have seen[26], and I am no chicken[27].'

'There is no clue[28]?' said Gregson.

'None at all,' chimed in Lestrade[29].

Sherlock Holmes approached the body, and, kneeling down, examined it intently[30]. 'You are sure that there is no wound?' he asked, pointing to numerous gouts and splashes[31] of blood which lay all round.

1. très bouclés
2. de plusieurs jours
3. de drap épais
4. redingote
5. gilet
6. manchettes
7. haut-de-forme
8. soigné
9. crispées
10. bras grands ouverts
11. jambes
12. entrecroisées
13. agonie
14. douloureuse
15. haine
16. malveillant
17. rictus
18. court
19. simiesque
20. convulsée
21. effrayant
22. crasseux
23. donnait sur
24. avec son habituelle allure de fouine
25. fera sensation
26. dépasse tout ce que j'ai pu voir
27. ne suis pas le perdreau de l'année
28. d'indice
29. répondit Lestrade en écho
30. avec attention
31. gouttes et éclaboussures

'Positive[1]!' cried both detectives.

'Then, of course, this blood belongs to a second individual — presumably the murderer, if murder has been committed. It reminds me of the circumstances attendant on[2] the death of Van Jansen, in Utrecht, in the year '34. Do you remember the case, Gregson?'

'No, sir.'

'Read it up — you really should. There is nothing new under the sun. It has all been done before.'

As he spoke, his nimble[3] fingers were flying here, there, and everywhere, feeling, pressing, unbuttoning, examining, while his eyes wore the same faraway expression which I have already remarked upon. So swiftly was the examination made, that one would hardly have guessed the minuteness[4] with which it was conducted. Finally, he sniffed the dead man's lips, and then glanced at the soles[5] of his patent leather[6] boots.

'He has not been moved at all?' he asked.

'No more than was necessary for the purposes[7] of our examination.'

'You can take him to the mortuary[8] now,' he said. 'There is nothing more to be learned.'

Gregson had a stretcher[9] and four men at hand. At his call they entered the room, and the stranger was lifted and carried out. As they raised him, a ring tinkled down[10] and rolled across the floor. Lestrade grabbed it up[11] and stared at it with mystified eyes[12].

'There's been a woman here,' he cried. 'It's a woman's wedding-ring.'

He held it out, as he spoke, upon the palm of his hand. We all gathered round him and gazed at it.

1. Absolument
2. associées à
3. agiles
4. précision
5. semelles
6. en cuir verni
7. besoins
8. morgue
9. civière
10. tomba en faisant entendre un tintement
11. s'en saisit
12. des yeux ébahis

There could be no doubt that that circlet[1] of plain gold had once adorned the finger of a bride.

'This complicates matters,' said Gregson. 'Heaven knows, they were complicated enough before.'

'You're sure it doesn't simplify them?' observed Holmes. 'There's nothing to be learned by staring at it[2]. What did you find in his pockets?'

'We have it all here,' said Gregson, pointing to a litter[3] of objects upon one of the bottom steps of the stairs. 'A gold watch, No. 97163, by Barraud, of London. Gold Albert chain[4], very heavy and solid. Gold ring, with masonic device[5]. Gold pin — bull-dog's head, with rubies as eyes. Russian leather card-case[6], with cards of Enoch J. Drebber of Cleveland, corresponding with the E.J.D. upon the linen. No purse, but loose money[7] to the extent of[8] seven pounds thirteen. Pocket edition of Boccaccio's *Decameron*, with name of Joseph Stangerson upon the fly-leaf[9]. Two letters — one addressed to E. J. Drebber and one to Joseph Stangerson.'

'At what address?'

'American Exchange, Strand — to be left till called for[10]. They are both from the Guion Steamship Company, and refer to the sailing of their boats from Liverpool. It is clear that this unfortunate man was about to return to New York.'

'Have you made any inquiries as to this man, Stangerson?'

'I did it at once, sir,' said Gregson. 'I have had advertisements sent[11] to all the newspapers, and one of my men has gone to the American Exchange, but he has not returned yet.'

'Have you sent to[12] Cleveland?'

'We telegraphed this morning.'

'How did you word your inquiries[13]?'

1. petit cercle
2. La fixer des yeux ne nous apprendra rien
3. petit tas
4. Une chaîne giletière
5. devise maçonnique
6. porte-cartes
7. de la petite monnaie
8. à hauteur de
9. page de garde
10. en poste restante
11. fait envoyer des petites annonces
12. écrit à
13. avez-vous formulé vos demandes de renseignements

'We simply detailed the circumstances, and said that we should be glad of any information which could help us.'

'You did not ask for particulars on any point[1] which appeared to you to be crucial[2]?'

'I asked about Stangerson.'

'Nothing else? Is there no circumstance on which this whole case appears to hinge[3]? Will you not telegraph again?'

'I have said all I have to say,' said Gregson, in an offended voice.

Sherlock Holmes chuckled to himself[4], and appeared to be about to make some remark, when Lestrade, who had been in the front room while we were holding this conversation in the hall, reappeared upon the scene, rubbing his hands in a pompous and self-satisfied manner[5].

'Mr. Gregson,' he said, 'I have just made a discovery of the highest importance, and one which would have been overlooked[6] had I not made a careful examination of the walls.'

The little man's eyes sparkled as he spoke, and he was evidently in a state of suppressed exultation[7] at having scored[8] a point against his colleague.

'Come here,' he said, bustling back[9] into the room, the atmosphere of which felt clearer[10] since the removal of its ghastly inmate[11]. 'Now, stand there!'

He struck a match on his boot and held it up against the wall.

'Look at that!' he said, triumphantly.

I have remarked[12] that the paper had fallen away in parts. In this particular corner of the room a large piece had peeled off[13], leaving a yellow square of coarse plastering[14]. Across this bare

1. des détails sur un point précis
2. particulièrement important
3. dépend
4. eut un petit rire sous cape
5. l'air prétentieux et très satisfait de lui-même
6. serait passée inaperçue
7. jubilation contenue
8. marqué
9. en retournant avec empressement
10. semblait assainie
11. épouvantable occupant
12. déjà fait remarquer
13. s'était détaché
14. plâtre brut

space there was scrawled[1] in blood-red letters a single word:

RACHE

'What do you think of that?' cried the detective, with the air of a showman exhibiting his show. 'This was overlooked because it was in the darkest corner of the room, and no one thought of looking there. The murderer has written it with his or her own blood. See this smear[2] where it has trickled[3] down the wall! That disposes of[4] the idea of suicide anyhow. Why was that corner chosen to write it on? I will tell you. See that candle on the mantelpiece. It was lit at the time, and if it was lit this corner would be the brightest instead of the darkest portion of the wall.'

'And what does it mean now that you *have* found it?' asked Gregson in a depreciatory voice[5].

'Mean? Why, it means that the writer was going to put the female name Rachel, but was disturbed before he or she had time to finish. You mark my words[6], when this case comes to be cleared up you will find that a woman named Rachel has something to do with it. It's all very well for you to laugh[7], Mr. Sherlock Holmes. You may be very smart and clever, but the old hound[8] is the best, when all is said and done[9].'

'I really beg your pardon!' said my companion, who had ruffled the little man's temper[10] by bursting into an explosion of laughter. 'You certainly have the credit[11] of being the first of us to find this out, and, as you say, it bears every mark of having been written[12] by the other participant in last night's mystery. I have not had time to examine

1. était griffonné
2. tache
3. le sang a goutté
4. écarte définitivement
5. sur un ton désobligeant
6. Retenez bien ce que je vous dis
7. Vous pouvez ricaner
8. limier
9. à la fin des fins
10. froissé le petit homme
11. le mérite
12. tout porte à croire que cette inscription a été faite

this room yet, but with your permission I shall do so now.'

As he spoke, he whipped[1] a tape measure[2] and a large round magnifying glass[3] from his pocket. With these two implements[4] he trotted noiselessly about the room, sometimes stopping, occasionally kneeling, and once lying flat upon his face. So engrossed[5] was he with his occupation that he appeared to have forgotten our presence, for he chattered away to himself under his breath[6] the whole time, keeping up a running fire[7] of exclamations, groans[8], whistles, and little cries suggestive of encouragement and of hope. As I watched him I was irresistibly reminded of a pure-blooded[9] well-trained foxhound[10] as it dashes backwards and forwards through the covert[11], whining in its eagerness[12], until it comes across the lost scent. For twenty minutes or more he continued his researches, measuring with the most exact care the distance between marks which were entirely invisible to me, and occasionally applying his tape to the walls in an equally incomprehensible manner. In one place he gathered up[13] very carefully a little pile of grey dust from the floor, and packed it away in an envelope. Finally, he examined with his glass the word upon the wall, going over every letter of it with the most minute exactness[14]. This done, he appeared to be satisfied, for[15] he replaced his tape and his glass in his pocket.

'They say that genius is an infinite capacity for taking pains[16],' he remarked with a smile. 'It's a very bad definition, but it does apply to detective work.'

Gregson and Lestrade had watched the manoeuvres of their amateur companion with

1. sortit prestement
2. mètre ruban
3. loupe
4. instruments,
5. absorbé
6. à voix basse
7. sous un tir nourri
8. de grognements
9. de race
10. chien de chasse
11. sillonnant le sous-bois en tous sens
12. gémissant d'impatience
13. ramassa
14. la plus grande minutie
15. car
16. à se donner du mal

considerable curiosity and some contempt[1]. They evidently failed to appreciate the fact[2], which I had begun to realize, that Sherlock Holmes' smallest actions were all directed towards some definite and practical end.

'What do you think of it, sir?' they both asked.

'It would be robbing you of the credit of the case if I was to presume[3] to help you,' remarked my friend. 'You are doing so well now that it would be a pity for anyone to interfere.' There was a world of[4] sarcasm in his voice as he spoke. 'If you will let me know how your investigations go,' he continued, 'I shall be happy to give you any help I can. In the meantime[5] I should like to speak to the constable who found the body. Can you give me his name and address?'

Lestrade glanced at his note-book. 'John Rance,' he said. 'He is off duty[6] now. You will find him at 46, Audley Court, Kennington Park Gate.'

Holmes took a note of the address.

'Come along, Doctor,' he said; 'we shall go and look him up[7]. I'll tell you one thing which may help you in the case,' he continued, turning to the two detectives. 'There has been murder done, and the murderer was a man. He was more than six feet high, was in the prime of life[8], had small feet for his height, wore coarse, square-toed boots[9] and smoked a Trichinopoly cigar. He came here with his victim in a four-wheeled cab, which was drawn by a horse with three old shoes[10] and one new one on his off fore leg[11]. In all probability the murderer had a florid face[12], and the finger-nails of his right hand were remarkably long. These are only a few indications, but they may assist you.'

1. quelque mépris
2. Manifestement ils ne saisissaient pas
3. me permettais
4. lourd
5. En attendant,
6. n'est pas de service
7. passer le voir
8. force de l'âge
9. des godillots à bouts carrés
10. fers
11. l'antérieur droit
12. teint rougeaud

Lestrade and Gregson glanced at each other with an incredulous smile.

'If this man was murdered, how was it done?' asked the former.

'Poison,' said Sherlock Holmes curtly[1], and strode off[2]. 'One other thing, Lestrade,' he added, turning round at the door: "Rache,' is the German for 'revenge;' so don't lose your time looking for Miss Rachel.'

With which Parthian shot[3] he walked away, leaving the two rivals open-mouthed[4] behind him.

1. sèchement
2. il partit à grands pas
3. Ayant lancé cette flèche du Parthe,
4. bouche bée

CHAPTER IV

What John Rance Had to Tell

IT was one o'clock when we left No. 3, Lauriston Gardens. Sherlock Holmes led me to the nearest telegraph office, whence[1] he dispatched a long telegram. He then hailed[2] a cab, and ordered the driver to take us to the address given us by Lestrade.

'There is nothing like first-hand evidence,' he remarked; 'as a matter of fact, my mind is entirely made up upon the case[3], but still we may as well learn all that is to be learned.'

'You amaze me, Holmes,' said I. 'Surely you are not as sure as you pretend to be of all those particulars which you gave.'

'There's no room for a mistake[4],' he answered. 'The very[5] first thing which I observed on arriving there was that a cab had made two ruts[6] with its wheels close to the curb[7]. Now, up to last night, we have had no rain for a week, so that those wheels which left such a deep impression must have been there during the night. There were the marks of the horse's hoofs[8], too, the outline of one of which[9] was far more clearly cut[10] than that of the other three, showing that that was a new shoe. Since the cab was there after the rain began, and was not there at any time during the morning — I have Gregson's word for that — it follows[11] that it must

1. d'où
2. héla
3. mon opinion sur l'affaire est déjà arrêtée
4. Il n'y a pas d'erreur possible
5. toute
6. creusé deux ornières
7. tout contre le trottoir
8. sabots
9. l'empreinte de l'un d'entre eux
10. se détachait beaucoup plus nettement
11. s'ensuit

have been there during the night, and, therefore, that it brought those two individuals to the house.'

'That seems simple enough,' said I; 'but how about the other man's height[1]?'

'Why, the height of a man, in nine cases out of ten, can be told from[2] the length of his stride[3]. It is a simple calculation enough, though there is no use[4] my boring you[5] with figures[6]. I had this fellow's stride both on the clay outside and on the dust within. Then I had a way of checking my calculation. When a man writes on a wall, his instinct leads him to write about the level of his own eyes. Now that writing was just over six feet[7] from the ground. It was child's play.'

'And his age?' I asked.

'Well, if a man can stride four and a-half feet[8] without the smallest effort, he can't be quite in the sere and yellow[9]. That was the breadth[10] of a puddle[11] on the garden walk which he had evidently walked across. Patent-leather boots had gone round[12], and Square-toes had hopped over[13]. There is no mystery about it at all. I am simply applying to ordinary life a few of those precepts of observation and deduction which I advocated[14] in that article. Is there anything else that puzzles you?'

'The finger nails and the Trichinopoly,' I suggested.

'The writing on the wall was done with a man's forefinger dipped in blood. My glass[15] allowed me to observe that the plaster was slightly scratched in doing it, which would not have been the case if the man's nail had been trimmed[16]. I gathered up some scattered ash from the floor. It was dark in colour and flakey[17] — such an ash as is only made by a Trichinopoly. I have made a special study of

1. taille
2. déduite de
3. enjambée
4. ce n'est pas la peine
5. que je vous ennuie
6. des chiffres
7. un peu plus de 1,80 m
8. enjamber près de 1,40 m
9. n'est sûrement pas à l'automne de sa vie
10. largeur
11. flaque d'eau
12. l'avaient contournée
13. sauté par-dessus
14. préconisais
15. loupe
16. bien limé
17. feuilletée

cigar ashes — in fact, I have written a monograph upon the subject. I flatter myself that I can distinguish at a glance the ash of any known brand[1], either of cigar or of tobacco. It is just in such details that the skilled detective differs from the Gregson and Lestrade type.'

'And the florid face?' I asked.

'Ah, that was a more daring shot[2], though I have no doubt that I was right. You must not ask me that at the present state of the affair.'

I passed my hand over my brow. 'My head is in a whirl[3],' I remarked; 'the more one thinks of it the more mysterious it grows. How came these two men — if there were two men — into an empty house? What has become of the cabman[4] who drove them? How could one man compel[5] another to take poison? Where did the blood come from? What was the object[6] of the murderer, since robbery had no part in it? How came the woman's ring there? Above all, why should the second man write up the German word RACHE before decamping? I confess that I cannot see any possible way of reconciling[7] all these facts.'

My companion smiled approvingly.

'You sum up[8] the difficulties of the situation succinctly and well,' he said. 'There is much that is still obscure, though I have quite made up my mind on the main facts. As to poor Lestrade's discovery it was simply a blind[9] intended to[10] put the police upon a wrong track[11], by suggesting Socialism and secret societies. It was not done by a German. The A, if you noticed, was printed somewhat after the German fashion[12]. Now, a real German invariably prints in the Latin character[13], so that we may safely say that this was not written by one, but by a

1. marque
2. hypothèse plus risquée
3. La tête me tourne
4. cocher
5. obliger
6. but
7. concilier
8. résumez
9. leurre
10. destiné à
11. fausse piste
12. se veut en caractère gothique
13. écrit en caractères latins

clumsy[1] imitator who overdid his part[2]. It was simply a ruse to divert[3] inquiry into a wrong channel. I'm not going to tell you much more of the case, Doctor. You know a conjuror[4] gets no credit[5] when once he has explained his trick, and if I show you too much of my method of working, you will come to the conclusion that I am a very ordinary individual after all.'

'I shall never do that,' I answered; 'you have brought detection[6] as near an exact science as it ever will be brought in this world.'

My companion flushed up with[7] pleasure at my words, and the earnest way in which[8] I uttered them[9]. I had already observed that he was as sensitive[10] to flattery on the score of[11] his art as any girl could be of her beauty.

'I'll tell you one other thing,' he said. 'Patent leathers and Square-toes came in the same cab, and they walked down the pathway together as friendly as possible — arm-in-arm[12], in all probability. When they got inside they walked up and down the room — or rather, Patent-leathers stood still while Square-toes walked up and down. I could read all that in the dust; and I could read that as he walked he grew more and more excited. That is shown by the increased[13] length of his strides. He was talking all the while, and working himself up[14], no doubt, into a fury[15]. Then the tragedy occurred. I've told you all I know myself now, for the rest is mere surmise[16] and conjecture. We have a good working basis, however, on which to start. We must hurry up, for I want to go to Hallé[17]'s concert to hear Norman-Neruda this afternoon.'

This conversation had occurred while our cab had been threading its way[18] through a long

1. mauvais
2. en a fait trop
3. orienter
4. prestidigitateur
5. n'a plus aucun mérite
6. l'art de l'investigation
7. rougit de
8. la conviction avec laquelle
9. je les avais prononcés
10. sensible
11. au sujet de
12. bras dessus bras dessous
13. croissante
14. s'énervait de plus en plus
15. jusqu'à être fou de rage
16. n'est que supposition
17. [Charles Hallé : pianiste et chef d'orchestre qui épousa la violoniste Wilma Norman-Neruda]
18. se frayait un chemin

succession of dingy[1] streets and dreary[2] by-ways[3]. In the dingiest and dreariest of them our driver suddenly came to a stand. 'That's Audley Court in there,' he said, pointing to a narrow slit in the line[4] of dead-coloured[5] brick. 'You'll find me here when you come back.'

Audley Court was not an attractive locality. The narrow passage led us into a quadrangle[6] paved with flags[7] and lined[8] by sordid dwellings. We picked our way[9] among groups of dirty children, and through lines[10] of discoloured linen, until we came to Number 46, the door of which was decorated with a small slip of brass[11] on which the name Rance was engraved. On enquiry we found[12] that the constable[13] was in bed, and we were shown[14] into a little front parlour to await his coming.

He appeared presently, looking a little irritable at being disturbed in his slumbers[15]. 'I made my report at the office,' he said.

Holmes took a half-sovereign from his pocket and played with it pensively. 'We thought that we should like to hear it all from your own lips,' he said.

'I shall be most happy to tell you anything I can,' the constable answered with his eyes upon the little golden disk.

'Just let us hear it all in your own way as it occurred.'

Rance sat down on the horsehair sofa[16], and knitted his brows[17] as though determined not to omit anything in his narrative.

'I'll tell it ye from the beginning,' he said. 'My time is[18] from ten at night to six in the morning. At eleven there was a fight at the White Hart[19]; but bar that[20] all was quiet enough on the beat[21]. At one

1. malpropres
2. tristes
3. ruelles
4. alignement
5. ternes
6. cour carrée
7. pavée
8. bordée
9. avançâmes prudemment
10. des rangées
11. plaque en laiton
12. On nous apprit
13. agent
14. on nous fit entrer
15. sommeil
16. canapé de crin
17. fronça les sourcils
18. Je suis de service
19. Cerf
20. à part ça,
21. pendant la ronde

o'clock it began to rain, and I met Harry Murcher — him who has the Holland Grove beat — and we stood together at the corner of Henrietta Street a-talkin'. Presently — maybe about two or a little after — I thought I would take a look round and see that all was right down the Brixton Road. It was precious dirty[1] and lonely[2]. Not a soul did I meet[3] all the way down[4], though a cab or two went past me. I was a-strollin' down[5], thinkin' between ourselves how uncommon handy a four of gin hot would be[6], when suddenly the glint of a light[7] caught my eye in the window of that same house. Now, I knew that them two houses in Lauriston Gardens was empty on account of him that owns them[8] who won't have the drains seen to[9], though the very last tenant[10] what[11] lived in one of them died o' typhoid fever. I was knocked all in a heap[12] therefore at seeing a light in the window, and I suspected as something was wrong. When I got to the door — '

'You stopped, and then walked back to the garden gate,' my companion interrupted. 'What did you do that for?[13]'

Rance gave a violent jump, and stared at Sherlock Holmes with the utmost amazement upon his features[14].

'Why, that's true, sir,' he said; 'though how you come to know it, Heaven only knows. Ye see, when I got up to the door it was so still and so lonesome[15], that I thought I'd be none the worse for[16] someone with me. I ain't afeared[17] of anything on this side o' the grave; but I thought that maybe it was him[18] that died o' the typhoid inspecting the drains[19] what[20] killed him. The thought gave me a kind o' turn[21], and I walked back to the gate to see

1. Il faisait un sale temps

2. c'était désert

3. J'ai croisé personne

4. sur toute la longueur de la rue

5. marchais tranquillement

6. qu'un petit un verre de gin chaud serait pas de refus

7. un rayon de lumière

8. à cause que leur proprio

9. veut pas faire réparer l'évacuation

10. locataire

11. [who]

12. surpris et pas qu'un peu

13. Pourquoi ça ?

14. effarement

15. calme et désert

16. que je ferais mieux d'avoir

17. [am not afraid]

18. celui

19. égouts

20. [that]

21. m'a filé un peu la pétoche

if I could see Murcher's lantern, but there wasn't no sign of him nor of anyone else.'

'There was no one in the street?'

'Not a livin' soul[1], sir, nor as much as a dog. Then I pulled myself together[2] and went back and pushed the door open. All was quiet inside, so I went into the room where the light was a-burnin'. There was a candle flickerin' on the mantelpiece — a red wax one — and by its light I saw — '

'Yes, I know all that you saw. You walked round the room several times, and you knelt down by the body, and then you walked through and tried the kitchen door, and then — '

John Rance sprang to his feet with a frightened face and suspicion in his eyes. 'Where was you hid to see all that?' he cried. 'It seems to me that you knows a deal more[3] than you should.'

Holmes laughed and threw his card across the table to the constable.

'Don't get arresting me for the murder,' he said. 'I am one of the hounds and not the wolf; Mr. Gregson or Mr. Lestrade will answer for that[4]. Go on, though. What did you do next?'

Rance resumed his seat[5], without however losing his mystified[6] expression. 'I went back to the gate and sounded my whistle[7]. That brought Murcher and two more to the spot.'

'Was the street empty then?'

'Well, it was, as far as anybody that could be of any good goes[8].'

'What do you mean?'

The constable's features broadened into a grin[9]. 'I've seen many a drunk chap[10] in my time,' he said, 'but never anyone so cryin' drunk as that cove[11]. He was at the gate when I came out, a-leanin' up

1. âme qui vive
2. je me suis repris
3. beaucoup plus
4. s'en porteront garants
5. se rassit
6. perplexe
7. j'ai donné des coups de sifflet
8. pour autant qu'on parle de gens convenables
9. se fendirent en un large sourire
10. beaucoup de gars soûls
11. d'aussi chargé que ce type

agin[1] the railings, and a-singin' at the pitch o' his lungs[2] about Columbine's New-fangled Banner[3], or some such stuff[4]. He couldn't stand[5], far less help[6].'

'What sort of a man was he?' asked Sherlock Holmes.

John Rance appeared to be somewhat irritated at this digression. 'He was an uncommon drunk sort o' man,' he said. 'He'd ha' found hisself[7] in the station[8] if we hadn't been so took up[9].'

'His face — his dress[10] — didn't you notice them?' Holmes broke in[11] impatiently.

'I should think I did notice them, seeing that I had to prop him up[12] — me and Murcher between us. He was a long chap, with a red face, the lower part muffled round[13] — '

'That will do[14],' cried Holmes. 'What became of him[15]?'

'We'd enough to do without lookin' after him,' the policeman said, in an aggrieved voice[16]. 'I'll wager[17] he found his way home all right.'

'How was he dressed?'

'A brown overcoat.'

'Had he a whip[18] in his hand?'

'A whip — no.'

'He must have left it behind,' muttered my companion. 'You didn't happen to see[19] or hear a cab after that?'

'No.'

'There's a half-sovereign for you,' my companion said, standing up and taking his hat. 'I am afraid, Rance, that you will never rise in the force[20]. That head of yours should be for use as well as ornament. You might have gained your sergeant's stripes[21] last night. The man whom you held in your hands is the man who holds the clue[22] of this

1. [against]
2. à pleins poumons
3. [Rance déforme les mots *Colombia* et *Star-Splangled Banner*, l'hymne américain]
4. un truc comme ça
5. tenir debout
6. encore moins donner un coup de main
7. [himself]
8. au poste
9. occupés
10. habillement
11. interrompit
12. vu que je devais le soutenir
13. emmitouflée
14. C'est bon
15. Qu'est-il devenu
16. d'un ton mécontent
17. Je parierais
18. fouet
19. n'auriez pas vu
20. que vous n'ayez jamais de promotion dans la police
21. galons
22. clé

mystery, and whom we are seeking. There is no use of arguing about it now; I tell you that it is so. Come along, Doctor.'

We started off for the cab together, leaving our informant[1] incredulous, but obviously uncomfortable.

'The blundering fool[2],' Holmes said, bitterly, as we drove back to our lodgings. 'Just to think of his having such an incomparable bit of good luck, and not taking advantage of it[3].'

'I am rather in the dark still[4]. It is true that the description of this man tallies with[5] your idea of the second party[6] in this mystery. But why should he come back to the house after leaving it? That is not the way of criminals.'

'The ring, man, the ring: that was what he came back for. If we have no other way of catching him, we can always bait our line[7] with the ring. I shall have him, Doctor — I'll lay you[8] two to one that I have him. I must thank you for it all. I might not have gone but for you[9], and so have missed[10] the finest study I ever came across: a study in scarlet, eh? Why shouldn't we use a little art jargon. There's the scarlet thread of murder running through the colourless skein[11] of life, and our duty is to unravel it[12], and isolate it, and expose every inch of it. And now for lunch[13], and then for[14] Norman-Neruda. Her attack and her bowing[15] are splendid. What's that little thing[16] of Chopin's she plays so magnificently: Tra-la-la-lira-lira-lay.'

Leaning back in the cab, this amateur bloodhound[17] carolled away like a lark[18] while I meditated upon the many-sidedness[19] of the human mind.

1. informateur
2. crétin
3. ne pas en profiter
4. n'y comprends toujours pas grand-chose
5. correspond à
6. homme impliqué
7. l'appâter
8. je vous parie
9. sans vous
10. j'aurais manqué ainsi
11. écheveau
12. de le démêler
13. allons déjeuner
14. allons écouter
15. coup d'archet
16. morceau
17. limier
18. fredonna gaiement
19. multiples facettes

CHAPTER V

Our Advertisement[1] *Brings a Visitor*

1. petite annonce

OUR morning's exertions[2] had been too much for my weak health, and I was tired out in the afternoon. After Holmes' departure for the concert, I lay down upon the sofa and endeavoured[3] to get a couple of hours' sleep. It was a useless attempt. My mind had been too much excited by all that had occurred, and the strangest fancies and surmises[4] crowded into it[5]. Every time that I closed my eyes I saw before me the distorted baboon-like[6] countenance[7] of the murdered man. So sinister was the impression which that face had produced upon me that I found it difficult to feel anything but gratitude for him who had removed its owner from the world. If ever human features bespoke[8] vice of the most malignant type[9], they were certainly those of Enoch J. Drebber, of Cleveland. Still I recognized that justice must be done, and that the depravity[10] of the victim was no condonement[11] in the eyes of the law.

The more I thought of it the more extraordinary did my companion's hypothesis, that the man had been poisoned, appear. I remembered how he had sniffed his lips, and had no doubt that he had detected something which had given rise to[12] the idea. Then, again, if not poison, what had caused the man's death, since there was neither wound

2. travaux
3. m'efforçai
4. hypothèses
5. y venaient en masse
6. de babouin
7. les traits
8. reflétèrent
9. le vice sous sa forme la plus malfaisante
10. turpitude
11. n'était pas une excuse
12. avait fait germer

nor marks of strangulation? But, on the other hand, whose blood was that which lay so thickly upon the floor? There were no signs of a struggle, nor had the victim any weapon with which he might have wounded an antagonist. As long as all these questions were unsolved[1], I felt that sleep would be no easy matter, either for Holmes or myself. His quiet self-confident manner[2] convinced me that he had already formed a theory which explained all the facts, though what it was I could not for an instant conjecture[3].

He was very late in returning — so late, that I knew that the concert could not have detained him[4] all the time. Dinner was on the table before he appeared.

'It was magnificent,' he said, as he took his seat. 'Do you remember what Darwin says about music? He claims[5] that the power of producing and appreciating it existed among the human race long before the power of speech was arrived at[6]. Perhaps that is why we are so subtly influenced by it. There are vague memories[7] in our souls of those misty[8] centuries when the world was in its childhood.'

'That's rather a broad[9] idea,' I remarked.

'One's ideas must be as broad as Nature if they are to interpret Nature,' he answered. 'What's the matter? You're not looking quite yourself[10]. This Brixton Road affair has upset you.'

'To tell the truth, it has,' I said. 'I ought to be more case-hardened[11] after my Afghan experiences. I saw my own comrades hacked to pieces[12] at Maiwand without losing my nerve[13].'

'I can understand. There is a mystery about this which stimulates the imagination; where there is

1. n'étaient pas résolues
2. attitude tranquille et confiante
3. n'en avais pas la moindre idée
4. l'avoir retenu
5. affirme
6. bien avant qu'il ne soit doué de parole
7. souvenirs
8. ténébreux
9. aventurée
10. n'avez pas l'air dans votre assiette
11. endurci
12. se faire tailler en pièces
13. perdre mon sang-froid

no imagination there is no horror. Have you seen the evening paper[1]?'

'No.'

'It gives a fairly good account[2] of the affair. It does not mention the fact that when the man was raised up, a woman's wedding ring fell upon the floor. It is just as well it does not.'

'Why?'

'Look at this advertisement[3],' he answered. 'I had one sent to every paper this morning immediately after the affair.'

He threw the paper across to me and I glanced at the place indicated. It was the first announcement in the 'Found[4]' column. 'In Brixton Road, this morning,' it ran[5], 'a plain gold wedding ring, found in the roadway[6] between the White Hart Tavern and Holland Grove. Apply[7] Dr. Watson, 221B, Baker Street, between eight and nine this evening.'

'Excuse my using your name,' he said. 'If I used my own some of these dunderheads[8] would recognize it, and want to meddle in[9] the affair.'

'That is all right,' I answered. 'But supposing anyone applies, I have no ring.'

'Oh yes, you have,' said he, handing me one[10]. 'This will do very well. It is almost a facsimile.'

'And who do you expect will answer this advertisement?'

'Why, the man in the brown coat — our florid friend with the square toes. If he does not come himself he will send an accomplice[11].'

'Would he not consider it as too dangerous?'

'Not at all. If my view of the case is correct, and I have every reason to believe that it is, this man would rather risk anything than lose the ring. According to my notion[12] he dropped it while

1. journal
2. rend assez bien compte
3. petite annonce
4. Objets trouvés
5. y lisait-on
6. sur la chaussée
7. S'adresser au
8. imbéciles
9. se mêler de
10. en m'en tendant une
11. complice
12. Selon moi,

1. en se penchant sur
2. il ne s'en est pas rendu compte sur le moment
3. déjà sur les lieux
4. grâce à la stupidité dont il avait fait preuve
5. écarter
6. impatiemment
7. tomberait sur
8. ravi
9. piège
10. le charger
11. aux abois
12. par surprise
13. il vaut mieux
14. débarrassée
15. s'adonnait à
16. Le mystère s'épaissit

stooping over[1] Drebber's body, and did not miss it at the time[2]. After leaving the house he discovered his loss and hurried back, but found the police already in possession[3], owing to his own folly[4] in leaving the candle burning. He had to pretend to be drunk in order to allay[5] the suspicions which might have been aroused by his appearance at the gate. Now put yourself in that man's place. On thinking the matter over, it must have occurred to him that it was possible that he had lost the ring in the road after leaving the house. What would he do, then? He would eagerly[6] look out for the evening papers in the hope of seeing it among the articles found. His eye, of course, would light upon[7] this. He would be overjoyed[8]. Why should he fear a trap[9]? There would be no reason in his eyes why the finding of the ring should be connected with the murder. He would come. He will come. You shall see him within an hour.'

'And then?' I asked.

'Oh, you can leave me to deal with him then. Have you any arms?'

'I have my old service revolver and a few cartridges.'

'You had better clean it and load it[10]. He will be a desperate man[11], and though I shall take him unawares[12], it is as well[13] to be ready for anything.'

I went to my bedroom and followed his advice. When I returned with the pistol the table had been cleared[14], and Holmes was engaged in[15] his favourite occupation of scraping upon his violin.

'The plot thickens[16],' he said, as I entered; 'I have just had an answer to my American telegram. My view of the case is the correct one.'

'And that is?' I asked eagerly.

'My fiddle would be the better for[1] new strings,' he remarked. 'Put your pistol in your pocket. When the fellow comes speak to him in an ordinary way. Leave the rest to me. Don't frighten him by looking at him too hard.'

'It is eight o'clock now,' I said, glancing at my watch.

'Yes. He will probably be here in a few minutes. Open the door slightly[2]. That will do. Now put the key on the inside. Thank you! This is a queer old book I picked up at a stall yesterday — *De Jure inter Gentes* — published in Latin at Liège in the Lowlands, in 1642. Charles' head was still firm on his shoulders[3] when this little brown-backed volume was struck off[4].'

'Who is the printer?'

'Philippe de Croy, whoever he may have been. On the fly-leaf, in very faded ink, is written 'Ex libris[5] Guliolmi Whyte.' I wonder who William Whyte was. Some pragmatical seventeenth century lawyer, I suppose. His writing has a legal twist about it[6]. Here comes our man, I think.'

As he spoke there was a sharp ring at the bell. Sherlock Holmes rose softly and moved his chair in the direction of the door. We heard the servant pass along the hall, and the sharp click[7] of the latch[8] as she opened it.

'Does Dr. Watson live here?' asked a clear but rather harsh[9] voice. We could not hear the servant's reply, but the door closed, and some one began to ascend the stairs. The footfall[10] was an uncertain and shuffling[11] one. A look of surprise passed over the face of my companion as he listened to it. It came slowly along the passage, and there was a feeble tap at the door.

1. violon s'accommoderait bien de
2. Entrebâillez la porte
3. [Charles 1er a été décapité en 1649]
4. est sorti
5. Livre appartenant à
6. quelque chose de juridique
7. déclic
8. loquet
9. criarde
10. bruit du pas
11. traînant

'Come in,' I cried.

At my summons[1], instead of the man of violence whom we expected, a very old and wrinkled[2] woman hobbled[3] into the apartment. She appeared to be dazzled[4] by the sudden blaze[5] of light, and after dropping a curtsey[6], she stood blinking at us with her bleared eyes[7] and fumbling[8] in her pocket with nervous, shaky fingers. I glanced at my companion, and his face had assumed such a disconsolate[9] expression that it was all I could do to keep my countenance[10].

The old crone[11] drew out an evening paper, and pointed at our advertisement. 'It's this as has brought me, good gentlemen,' she said, dropping another curtsey; 'a gold wedding ring in the Brixton Road. It belongs to my girl Sally, as was married only this time twelvemonth[12], which her[13] husband is steward aboard a Union boat, and what he'd say if he come 'ome[14] and found her without her ring is more than I can think[15], he being short enough[16] at the best o' times[17], but more especially when he has the drink[18]. If it please you, she went to the circus last night along with — '

'Is that her ring?' I asked.

'The Lord be thanked!' cried the old woman; 'Sally will be a glad woman this night. That's the ring.'

'And what may your address be?' I inquired, taking up a pencil.

'13, Duncan Street, Houndsditch. A weary way[19] from here.'

'The Brixton Road does not lie between any circus and Houndsditch,' said Sherlock Holmes sharply.

1. injonction
2. ridée
3. entra en boitillant
4. éblouie
5. éclat
6. avoir fait une révérence
7. se tint devant nous, ses yeux troubles papillotant
8. et elle tâtonnait
9. affligée
10. j'eus un mal fou à garder mon sérieux
11. La vieille bonne femme
12. y a juste un an de ça
13. [whose]
14. [home]
15. j'ose pas y penser
16. déjà qu'il s'énerve facilement
17. en temps normal
18. un verre dans le nez
19. Un sacré bout de chemin

The old woman faced round and looked keenly at him[1] from her little red-rimmed[2] eyes. 'The gentleman asked me for *my* address,' she said. 'Sally lives in lodgings at 3, Mayfield Place, Peckham.'

'And your name is — ?'

'My name is Sawyer — her's is Dennis, which Tom Dennis married her — and a smart, clean lad, too, as long as he's at sea, and no steward in the company more thought of[3]; but when on shore[4], what with the women[5] and what with liquor shops[6] — '

'Here is your ring, Mrs. Sawyer,' I interrupted, in obedience to[7] a sign from my companion; 'it clearly belongs to your daughter, and I am glad to be able to restore it[8] to the rightful owner[9].'

With many mumbled blessings[10] and protestations of gratitude the old crone packed it away in her pocket, and shuffled off[11] down the stairs. Sherlock Holmes sprang to his feet the moment that she was gone and rushed into his room. He returned in a few seconds enveloped in an ulster[12] and a cravat[13]. 'I'll follow her,' he said, hurriedly; 'she must be an accomplice, and will lead me to him. Wait up for me.' The hall door had hardly slammed[14] behind our visitor before Holmes had descended the stair. Looking through the window I could see her walking feebly along the other side, while her pursuer dogged her[15] some little distance behind. 'Either his whole theory is incorrect,' I thought to myself, 'or else he will be led now to the heart of the mystery.' There was no need for him to ask me to wait up for him, for I felt that sleep was impossible until I heard the result of his adventure.

It was close upon nine when he set out. I had no idea how long he might be, but I sat stolidly[16]

1. le fixa d'un regard perçant
2. cernés de rouge
3. apprécié
4. il est à terre
5. avec les femmes d'un côté
6. les troquets de l'autre
7. en réponse à
8. la restituer
9. à son légitime propriétaire
10. Tout en marmonnant force bénédictions
11. repartit de son pas traînant
12. pardessus
13. foulard
14. claqué
15. la filait
16. je l'attendis stoïquement

puffing at[1] my pipe and skipping over the pages of[2] Henri Murger's *Vie de Bohème.* Ten o'clock passed, and I heard the footsteps of the maid as they pattered off to bed[3]. Eleven, and the more stately tread[4] of the landlady passed my door, bound for[5] the same destination. It was close upon twelve before I heard the sharp sound of his latch-key. The instant he entered I saw by his face that he had not been successful. Amusement and chagrin[6] seemed to be struggling for the mastery[7], until the former suddenly carried the day[8], and he burst into a hearty laugh.

'I wouldn't have the Scotland Yarders know it for the world[9],' he cried, dropping into his chair; 'I have chaffed them so much[10] that they would never have let me hear the end of it. I can afford to laugh, because I know that I will be even with them[11] in the long run.'

'What is it then?' I asked.

'Oh, I don't mind telling a story against myself. That creature had gone a little way when she began to limp[12] and show every sign of being footsore[13]. Presently she came to a halt, and hailed a four-wheeler[14] which was passing. I managed to be close to her so as to hear the address, but I need not have been so anxious[15], for she sang it out loud enough[16] to be heard at the other side of the street, 'Drive to 13, Duncan Street, Houndsditch,' she cried. This begins to look genuine[17], I thought, and having seen her safely inside[18], I perched myself behind. That's an art which every detective should be an expert at. Well, away we rattled, and never drew rein[19] until we reached the street in question. I hopped off[20] before we came to the door, and strolled down[21] the street in an

1. en tirant sur
2. parcourant distraitement
3. les petits pas de la servante partant se coucher
4. le pas plus imposant
5. en route pour
6. la contrariété
7. se disputer l'avantage
8. l'emporte
9. ne voudrais pour rien au monde que Scotland Yard soit au courant
10. les ai tellement raillés
11. prendrai ma revanche
12. boiter
13. à avoir clairement mal au pied
14. fiacre
15. de me donner tant de mal
16. car elle l'annonça suffisamment fort
17. véridique
18. l'ayant bien vue s'installer à l'intérieur
19. sans marquer aucun arrêt
20. ai sauté à terre
21. j'ai longé

easy, lounging way[1]. I saw the cab pull up[2]. The driver jumped down, and I saw him open the door and stand expectantly[3]. Nothing came out though. When I reached him he was groping about frantically[4] in the empty cab, and giving vent to[5] the finest assorted collection of oaths[6] that ever I listened to. There was no sign or trace of his passenger, and I fear it will be some time before he gets his fare[7]. On inquiring at Number 13 we found that the house belonged to a respectable paperhanger[8], named Keswick, and that no one of the name either of Sawyer or Dennis had ever been heard of there.'

'You don't mean to say,' I cried, in amazement, 'that that tottering[9], feeble old woman was able to get out of the cab while it was in motion, without either you or the driver seeing her?'

'Old woman be damned!' said Sherlock Holmes, sharply. 'We were the old women to be so taken in[10]. It must have been a young man, and an active one, too, besides being an incomparable actor. The get-up[11] was inimitable[12]. He saw that he was followed, no doubt, and used this means of giving me the slip[13]. It shows that the man we are after is not as lonely as I imagined he was, but has friends who are ready to risk something for him. Now, Doctor, you are looking done-up[14]. Take my advice and turn in[15].'

I was certainly feeling very weary[16], so I obeyed his injunction. I left Holmes seated in front of the smouldering fire[17], and long into the watches of the night[18] I heard the low, melancholy wailings[19] of his violin, and knew that he was still pondering over[20] the strange problem which he had set himself to unravel[21].

1. avec nonchalance
2. s'arrêter
3. attendre
4. cherchait frénétiquement à tâtons
5. laissant échapper
6. bordée de jurons
7. le prix de sa course
8. tapissier
9. chancelante
10. pour nous laisser berner de la sorte
11. L'accoutrement
12. exceptionnel
13. pour me filer entre les doigts
14. éreinté
15. allez vous coucher
16. las
17. feu qui se consumait lentement
18. très avant dans la nuit
19. plaintes
20. qu'il songeait toujours à
21. qu'il s'était donné pour tâche de résoudre

CHAPTER VI

Tobias Gregson Shows What He Can Do

THE papers next day were full of the 'Brixton Mystery,' as they termed it[1]. Each had a long account of the affair, and some had leaders upon it in addition[2]. There was some information in them which was new to me. I still retain in my scrap-book numerous clippings[3] and extracts bearing upon[4] the case. Here is a condensation[5] of a few of them:

The *Daily Telegraph* remarked that in the history of crime there had seldom been a tragedy which presented stranger features. The German name of the victim, the absence of all other motive, and the sinister inscription on the wall, all pointed to its perpetration[6] by political refugees and revolutionists. The Socialists had many branches in America, and the deceased[7] had, no doubt, infringed[8] their unwritten laws[9], and been tracked down[10] by them. After alluding airily to[11] the Vehmgericht[12], acqua tofana[13], Carbonari[14], the Marchioness[15] de Brinvilliers, the Darwinian theory, the principles of Malthus, and the Ratcliff Highway murders, the article concluded by admonishing[16] the Government and advocating[17] a closer watch over[18] foreigners in England.

The *Standard* commented upon the fact that lawless outrages of the sort usually occurred under

1. comme ils l'appelaient
2. certains y consacraient même leur éditorial
3. coupures
4. concernant
5. résumé
6. tout indiquait qu'il avait été perpétré
7. défunt
8. enfreint
9. règles tacites
10. dépisté
11. avoir évoqué sans y toucher
12. Sainte-Vehme [société secrète de l'Allemagne médiévale]
13. [poison célèbre en Italie]
14. [société secrète italienne]
15. marquise [criminelle française]
16. en tançant
17. en préconisant
18. qu'on surveille de plus près

a Liberal Administration[1]. They arose[2] from the unsettling[3] of the minds of the masses, and the consequent[4] weakening[5] of all authority. The deceased was an American gentleman who had been residing for some weeks in the Metropolis[6]. He had stayed at the boarding-house[7] of Madame Charpentier, in Torquay Terrace, Camberwell. He was accompanied in his travels by his private secretary, Mr. Joseph Stangerson. The two bade adieu[8] to their landlady upon Tuesday, the 4th inst.[9], and departed to Euston Station with the avowed[10] intention of catching the Liverpool express. They were afterwards seen together upon the platform[11]. Nothing more is known of them until Mr. Drebber's body was, as recorded[12], discovered in an empty house in the Brixton Road, many miles from Euston. How he came there, or how he met his fate[13], are questions which are still involved in[14] mystery. Nothing is known of the whereabouts of[15] Stangerson. We are glad to learn that Mr. Lestrade and Mr. Gregson, of Scotland Yard, are both engaged upon the case[16], and it is confidently anticipated[17] that these well-known officers will speedily throw light upon the matter[18].

The *Daily News* observed that there was no doubt as to the crime being a political one. The despotism and hatred of Liberalism which animated[19] the Continental Governments had had the effect of driving to our shores a number of men who might have made excellent citizens were they not soured[20] by the recollection[21] of all that they had undergone[22]. Among these men there was a stringent[23] code of honour, any infringement[24] of which was punished by death. Every effort should be made to find the secretary, Stangerson, and to

1. gouvernement
2. résultaient
3. déstabilisation
4. et de son corollaire,
5. l'affaiblissement
6. la capitale
7. pension de famille
8. avaient pris congé de
9. le mardi 4 courant
10. déclarée
11. quai
12. comme nous l'avons dit
13. a connu ce sort funeste
14. entourées de mystère
15. lieu où se trouve
16. chargés de l'affaire
17. nous escomptons en toute confiance
18. ne tarderont pas à élucider l'affaire
19. inspiraient
20. aigris
21. souvenir
22. subi
23. rigoureux
24. violation

ascertain[1] some particulars[2] of the habits[3] of the deceased. A great step had been gained by the discovery of the address of the house at which he had boarded[4] — a result which was entirely due to the acuteness[5] and energy of Mr. Gregson of Scotland Yard.

Sherlock Holmes and I read these notices over together at breakfast, and they appeared to afford him[6] considerable amusement.

'I told you that, whatever happened, Lestrade and Gregson would be sure to score[7].'

'That depends on how it turns out[8].'

'Oh, bless you[9], it doesn't matter in the least[10]. If the man is caught, it will be *on account* of[11] their exertions[12]; if he escapes, it will be *in spite* of[13] their exertions. It's heads I win and tails you lose[14]. Whatever they do, they will have followers[15]. "Un sot trouve toujours un plus sot qui l'admire." '

'What on earth is this?' I cried, for at this moment there came the pattering of many steps[16] in the hall and on the stairs, accompanied by audible expressions of disgust upon the part of our landlady.

'It's the Baker Street division of the detective police force,' said my companion, gravely; and as he spoke there rushed into the room half a dozen of the dirtiest and most ragged[17] street Arabs[18] that ever I clapped eyes on[19].

' 'Tention![20]' cried Holmes, in a sharp tone, and the six dirty little scoundrels[21] stood in a line like so many[22] disreputable[23] statuettes. 'In future you shall send up Wiggins alone to report[24], and the rest of you must wait in the street. Have you found it, Wiggins?'

'No, sir, we hain't[25],' said one of the youths.

1. vérifier
2. certains détails
3. quant aux habitudes
4. pris pension
5. perspicacité
6. lui procurer
7. à coup sûr les gagnants
8. de comment les choses tournent
9. mon Dieu
10. n'a aucune importance
11. *grâce à*
12. leur acharnement
13. *malgré*
14. face je gagne, pile tu perds
15. des partisans
16. on entendit le bruit de nombreux pas qui trottinaient
17. loqueteux
18. gamins des rues
19. que j'eusse jamais vus
20. Garde-à-vous !
21. garnements
22. autant de
23. peu recommandables
24. au rapport
25. [haven't]

'I hardly expected you would. You must keep on until you do. Here are your wages[1].' He handed each of them a shilling. 'Now, off you go[2], and come back with a better report next time.'

He waved his hand, and they scampered away downstairs[3] like so many rats, and we heard their shrill[4] voices next moment in the street.

'There's more work to be got out of one of those little beggars[5] than out of a dozen of the force[6],' Holmes remarked. 'The mere sight[7] of an official-looking person seals men's lips. These youngsters, however, go everywhere and hear everything. They are as sharp as needles[8], too; all they want[9] is organisation.'

'Is it on this Brixton case that you are employing them?' I asked.

'Yes; there is a point which I wish to ascertain. It is merely a matter of time. Hullo! we are going to hear some news now with a vengeance[10]! Here is Gregson coming down the road with beatitude written upon every feature of his face. Bound for us, I know[11]. Yes, he is stopping. There he is!'

There was a violent peal at the bell[12], and in a few seconds the fair-haired detective came up the stairs, three steps at a time, and burst into our sitting-room.

'My dear fellow,' he cried, wringing Holmes' unresponsive hand[13], 'congratulate me! I have made the whole thing as clear as day.'

A shade of anxiety seemed to me to cross my companion's expressive face.

'Do you mean that you are on the right track?' he asked.

'The right track! Why, sir, we have the man under lock and key[14].'

1. paye
2. allez-vous-en
3. détalèrent dans l'escalier
4. aiguës
5. Un seul de ces petits mendiants est plus ardent à la tâche
6. qu'une douzaine de policiers
7. seule vue
8. très futés
9. tout ce qui leur manque
10. de fortes nouvelles
11. Il vient nous voir, j'en suis sûr
12. La sonnette retentit impérieusement
13. en serrant la main inerte de Holmes
14. sous les verrous

'And his name is?'

'Arthur Charpentier, sub-lieutenant in Her Majesty's navy,' cried Gregson, pompously, rubbing his fat hands and inflating his chest[1].

Sherlock Holmes gave a sigh of relief[2], and relaxed into a smile.

'Take a seat, and try one of these cigars,' he said. 'We are anxious[3] to know how you managed it. Will you have some whiskey and water?'

'I don't mind if I do[4],' the detective answered. 'The tremendous exertions[5] which I have gone through[6] during the last day or two have worn me out. Not so much bodily[7] exertion, you understand, as the strain upon the mind[8]. You will appreciate that[9], Mr. Sherlock Holmes, for we are both brain-workers[10].'

'You do me too much honour,' said Holmes, gravely. 'Let us hear how you arrived at this most gratifying[11] result.'

The detective seated himself in the arm-chair, and puffed complacently at[12] his cigar. Then suddenly he slapped his thigh in a paroxysm of amusement.

'The fun of it is,' he cried, 'that that fool Lestrade, who thinks himself so smart, has gone off upon the wrong track altogether[13]. He is after[14] the secretary Stangerson, who had no more to do with the crime than the babe unborn. I have no doubt that he has caught him by this time.'

The idea tickled Gregson so much[15] that he laughed until he choked[16].

'And how did you get your clue?'

'Ah, I'll tell you all about it. Of course, Doctor Watson, this is strictly between ourselves. The first difficulty which we had to contend with[17] was

1. gonflant la poitrine
2. poussa un soupir de soulagement
3. impatients
4. Ce n'est pas de refus
5. formidables efforts
6. que j'ai consentis
7. physique
8. tension psychologique
9. comprenez cela sans doute
10. travaillons tous deux avec notre cervelle
11. très satisfaisant
12. tout content de lui, tira sur
13. se fourvoie complètement
14. recherche
15. réjouissait tellement Gregson
16. qu'il rit à s'en étouffer
17. à laquelle il nous fallut faire face

the finding of this American's antecedents. Some people would have waited until their advertisements were answered, or until parties[1] came forward[2] and volunteered[3] information. That is not Tobias Gregson's way of going to work. You remember the hat beside the dead man?'

'Yes,' said Holmes; 'by John Underwood and Sons, 129, Camberwell Road.'

Gregson looked quite crestfallen[4].

'I had no idea that you noticed that,' he said. 'Have you been there?'

'No.'

'Ha!' cried Gregson, in a relieved[5] voice; 'you should never neglect a chance, however small it may seem.'

'To a great mind, nothing is little,' remarked Holmes, sententiously.

'Well, I went to Underwood, and asked him if he had sold a hat of that size and description. He looked over his books[6], and came on it at once. He had sent the hat to a Mr. Drebber, residing at Charpentier's Boarding Establishment, Torquay Terrace. Thus I got at his address.'

'Smart — very smart!' murmured Sherlock Holmes.

'I next called upon Madame Charpentier,' continued the detective. 'I found her very pale and distressed. Her daughter was in the room, too — an uncommonly fine girl she is, too; she was looking red about the eyes and her lips trembled as I spoke to her. That didn't escape my notice[7]. I began to smell a rat[8]. You know the feeling[9], Mr. Sherlock Holmes, when you come upon the right scent — a kind of thrill in your nerves[10]. "Have you heard

1. ou jusqu'à ce que quelqu'un
2. se présente
3. livre
4. eut l'air tout déconfit
5. soulagée
6. a consulté ses registres
7. Ce qui ne m'a pas échappé
8. Ça sentait l'embrouille
9. sensation
10. petit frisson qui vous électrise

of the mysterious death of your late boarder[1] Mr. Enoch J. Drebber, of Cleveland?" I asked.

'The mother nodded[2]. She didn't seem able to get out a word. The daughter burst into tears. I felt more than ever that these people knew something of the matter.

' "At what o'clock[3] did Mr. Drebber leave your house for the train?" I asked.

' "At eight o'clock," she said, gulping in her throat[4] to keep down[5] her agitation. "His secretary, Mr. Stangerson, said that there were two trains — one at 9.15 and one at 11. He was to catch the first."

' "And was that the last which you saw of him[6]?"

'A terrible change came over the woman's face as I asked the question. Her features turned perfectly livid. It was some seconds before she could get out the single word "Yes" — and when it did come it was in a husky unnatural tone[7].

'There was silence for a moment, and then the daughter spoke in a calm clear voice.

' "No good can ever come of falsehood[8], mother," she said. "Let us be frank with this gentleman. We *did* see Mr. Drebber again."

' "God forgive you!" cried Madame Charpentier, throwing up her hands and sinking back[9] in her chair. "You have murdered your brother."

' "Arthur would rather that we spoke the truth," the girl answered firmly.

' "You had best tell me all about it now," I said. "Half-confidences are worse than none[10]. Besides, you do not know how much we know of it."

' "On your head be it[11], Alice!" cried her mother; and then, turning to me, "I will tell you all, sir. Do not imagine that my agitation[12] on behalf of[13] my son arises from any fear[14] lest he should have had

1. défunt pensionnaire
2. acquiesça
3. À quelle heure
4. et elle déglutissait
5. pour dominer
6. vous ne l'avez pas revu depuis
7. d'une étrange voix rauque
8. Il ne peut rien sortir de bon d'un mensonge
9. en se laissant retomber
10. Ne parler qu'à moitié est pire que se taire
11. Tu en assumeras les conséquences
12. trouble
13. concernant
14. résulte de la peur

a hand[1] in this terrible affair. He is utterly innocent of it. My dread is[2], however, that in your eyes and in the eyes of others he may appear to be compromised. That however is surely impossible. His high character[3], his profession, his antecedents would all forbid it[4]."

' "Your best way is to make a clean breast of the facts[5]," I answered. "Depend upon it[6], if your son is innocent he will be none the worse[7]."

' "Perhaps, Alice, you had better leave us together," she said, and her daughter withdrew. "Now, sir," she continued, "I had no intention of telling you all this, but since my poor daughter has disclosed it[8] I have no alternative[9]. Having once decided to speak, I will tell you all without omitting any particular[10]."

' "It is your wisest course[11]," said I.

' "Mr. Drebber has been with us nearly three weeks. He and his secretary, Mr. Stangerson, had been travelling on the Continent. I noticed a 'Copenhagen' label[12] upon each of their trunks, showing that that had been their last stopping place. Stangerson was a quiet reserved man, but his employer, I am sorry to say, was far otherwise[13]. He was coarse in his habits[14] and brutish in his ways[15]. The very night[16] of his arrival he became very much the worse for drink[17], and, indeed, after twelve o'clock in the day he could hardly ever be said to be sober. His manners towards the maid-servants were disgustingly free and familiar[18]. Worst of all, he speedily assumed[19] the same attitude towards my daughter, Alice, and spoke to her more than once in a way which, fortunately, she is too innocent to understand. On one occasion he actually seized her[20] in his arms and embraced her

1. qu'il ait pu tremper
2. Ce que je crains
3. haute moralité
4. tout cela s'y oppose
5. de tout avouer
6. Croyez-moi
7. n'en pâtira pas
8. l'a révélé,
9. n'ai pas le choix
10. détail
11. le plus sage
12. étiquette
13. bien différent
14. Sa conduite était grossière
15. ses manières, brutales
16. Le soir même
17. a bu bien plus que de raison
18. d'une impudence et d'une familiarité répugnantes
19. a rapidement adopté
20. est allé jusqu'à la prendre

— an outrage which caused his own secretary to reproach him for his unmanly[1] conduct."

' "But why did you stand[2] all this," I asked. "I suppose that you can get rid of your boarders when you wish."

'Madame Charpentier blushed at my pertinent question. "Would to God that I had given him notice[3] on the very day that he came," she said. "But it was a sore[4] temptation. They were paying a pound a day each — fourteen pounds a week, and this is the slack season[5]. I am a widow[6], and my boy in the Navy has cost me much. I grudged[7] to lose the money. I acted for the best[8]. This last was too much, however, and I gave him notice to leave on account of it[9]. That was the reason of his going."

' "Well?"

' "My heart grew light when I saw him drive away. My son is on leave[10] just now, but I did not tell him anything of all this, for his temper is violent, and he is passionately fond of his sister. When I closed the door behind them a load[11] seemed to be lifted from my mind. Alas, in less than an hour there was a ring at the bell, and I learned that Mr. Drebber had returned. He was much excited, and evidently the worse for drink. He forced his way into the room, where I was sitting with my daughter, and made some incoherent remark about having missed his train. He then turned to Alice, and before my very face[12], proposed to her that she should fly with him[13]. 'You are of age[14],' he said, 'and there is no law to stop you. I have money enough and to spare[15]. Never mind the old girl here[16], but come along with me now straight away. You shall live like a princess.' Poor Alice was so frightened that she shrunk away from him, but he

1. honteuse
2. avez-vous supporté
3. Si seulement je lui avais donné congé
4. terrible
5. saison creuse
6. veuve
7. rechignais
8. J'ai cru agir pour le mieux
9. pour cette raison
10. en permission
11. grand poids
12. sous mes yeux
13. de s'enfuir avec lui
14. majeure
15. plus qu'assez d'argent
16. Peu importe la vieille

caught her by the wrist and endeavoured to draw her towards the door. I screamed, and at that moment my son Arthur came into the room. What happened then I do not know. I heard oaths and the confused sounds of a scuffle[1]. I was too terrified to raise my head. When I did look up I saw Arthur standing in the doorway laughing, with a stick in his hand. 'I don't think that fine fellow will trouble us again,' he said. 'I will just go after him and see what he does with himself[2].' With those words he took his hat and started off down the street. The next morning we heard of Mr. Drebber's mysterious death."

'This statement[3] came from Madame Charpentier's lips with many gasps[4] and pauses. At times she spoke so low that I could hardly catch the words. I made shorthand notes[5] of all that she said, however, so that there should be no possibility of a mistake.'

'It's quite exciting,' said Sherlock Holmes, with a yawn[6]. 'What happened next?'

'When Madame Charpentier paused,' the detective continued, 'I saw that the whole case hung upon one point. Fixing her with my eye in a way which I always found effective[7] with women, I asked her at what hour her son returned.

' "I do not know," she answered.

' "Not know?"

' "No; he has a latch-key, and he let himself in[8]."

' "After you went to bed?"

' "Yes."

' "When did you go to bed?"

' "About eleven."

' "So your son was gone at least two hours?"

' "Yes."

1. bagarre

2. pour voir où il va

3. déclaration

4. hoquets

5. des notes en sténo

6. en bâillant

7. efficace

8. n'a pas eu besoin qu'on lui ouvre

' "Possibly four or five?"

' "Yes."

' "What was he doing during that time?"

' "I do not know," she answered, turning white to her very lips[1].

'Of course after that there was nothing more to be done. I found out where Lieutenant Charpentier was, took two officers[2] with me, and arrested him. When I touched him on the shoulder and warned him to come quietly with us, he answered us as bold as brass[3], 'I suppose you are arresting me for being concerned[4] in the death of that scoundrel[5] Drebber,' he said. We had said nothing to him about it, so that his alluding to it[6] had a most suspicious aspect.'

'Very,' said Holmes.

'He still carried the heavy stick which the mother described him as having with him when he followed Drebber. It was a stout oak cudgel[7].'

'What is your theory, then?'

'Well, my theory is that he followed Drebber as far as the Brixton Road. When there, a fresh[8] altercation arose between them[9], in the course of which Drebber received a blow from the stick, in the pit of the stomach[10], perhaps, which killed him without leaving any mark. The night was so wet that no one was about[11], so Charpentier dragged the body of his victim into the empty house. As to the candle, and the blood, and the writing on the wall, and the ring, they may all be so many tricks[12] to throw the police on to the wrong scent.'

'Well done!' said Holmes in an encouraging voice. 'Really, Gregson, you are getting along[13]. We shall make something of you yet.'

1. et elle devint absolument livide
2. agents
3. avec un aplomb incroyable
4. en raison de mon implication dans
5. cette crapule de
6. qu'il y fasse donc allusion
7. solide gourdin de chêne
8. nouvelle
9. les a opposés
10. en plein dans l'abdomen
11. qu'il n'y avait personne
12. autant de ruses
13. faites des progrès

'I flatter myself that I have managed it rather neatly[1],' the detective answered proudly. 'The young man volunteered a statement[2], in which he said that after following Drebber some time, the latter perceived him[3], and took a cab in order to get away from him. On his way home he met an old shipmate[4], and took a long walk with him. On being asked where this old shipmate lived, he was unable to give any satisfactory reply. I think the whole case fits together uncommonly well[5]. What amuses me is to think of Lestrade, who had started off upon the wrong scent. I am afraid he won't make much of it[6]. Why, by Jove, here's the very man himself[7]!'

It was indeed Lestrade, who had ascended the stairs while we were talking, and who now entered the room. The assurance and jauntiness[8] which generally marked his demeanour and dress[9] were, however, wanting[10]. His face was disturbed and troubled, while his clothes were disarranged and untidy. He had evidently come with the intention of consulting[11] with Sherlock Holmes, for on perceiving[12] his colleague he appeared to be embarrassed and put out[13]. He stood in the centre of the room, fumbling nervously with[14] his hat and uncertain what to do[15]. 'This is a most extraordinary case,' he said at last — 'a most incomprehensible affair.'

'Ah, you find it so, Mr. Lestrade!' cried Gregson, triumphantly. 'I thought you would come to that conclusion. Have you managed to find the secretary, Mr. Joseph Stangerson?'

'The secretary, Mr. Joseph Stangerson,' said Lestrade gravely, 'was murdered at Halliday's Private Hotel about six o'clock this morning.'

1. rondement
2. a fait une déclaration
3. ce dernier l'avait repéré
4. un ancien compagnon de bord
5. que tous les éléments se combinent parfaitement
6. Il n'en tirera pas grand-chose, malheureusement
7. le voici en personne
8. assurance enjouée
9. caractérisaient sa conduite et sa façon de s'habiller
10. faisaient cependant défaut
11. s'entretenir
12. en voyant
13. contrarié
14. triturant nerveusement
15. ne sachant trop que faire

CHAPTER VII

Light in the Darkness

1. information
2. capitale
3. stupéfaits
4. renversa
5. bégaya
6. point de vue
7. veux bien admettre
8. Acquis à cette idée
9. j'ai voulu savoir

THE intelligence[1] with which Lestrade greeted us was so momentous[2] and so unexpected, that we were all three fairly dumfounded[3]. Gregson sprang out of his chair and upset[4] the remainder of his whiskey and water. I stared in silence at Sherlock Holmes, whose lips were compressed and his brows drawn down over his eyes.

'Stangerson too!' he muttered. 'The plot thickens.'

'It was quite thick enough before,' grumbled Lestrade, taking a chair. 'I seem to have dropped into a sort of council of war.'

'Are you — are you sure of this piece of intelligence?' stammered[5] Gregson.

'I have just come from his room,' said Lestrade. 'I was the first to discover what had occurred.'

'We have been hearing Gregson's view[6] of the matter,' Holmes observed. 'Would you mind letting us know what you have seen and done?'

'I have no objection,' Lestrade answered, seating himself. 'I freely confess[7] that I was of the opinion that Stangerson was concerned in the death of Drebber. This fresh development has shown me that I was completely mistaken. Full of the one idea[8], I set myself to find out[9] what had become of the Secretary. They had been seen together at Euston Station about half-past eight on the evening of the third[1]. At two in the morning Drebber had been found in the Brixton Road. The question which confronted me was to find out how Stangerson had been employed between 8.30 and the time of the crime, and what had become of him afterwards. I telegraphed to Liverpool, giving a description of the man, and warning them to keep a watch upon[2] the American boats. I then set to work calling upon all the hotels and lodging-houses in the vicinity[3] of Euston. You see, I argued[4] that if Drebber and his companion had become separated, the natural course[5] for the latter would be to put up[6] somewhere in the vicinity for the night, and then to hang about the station[7] again next morning.'

'They would be likely to agree on some meeting-place[8] beforehand[9],' remarked Holmes.

'So it proved. I spent the whole of yesterday evening in making enquiries entirely without avail[10]. This morning I began very early, and at eight o'clock I reached Halliday's Private Hotel, in Little George Street. On my enquiry as to whether[11] a Mr. Stangerson was living there, they at once answered me in the affirmative.

' "No doubt you are the gentleman whom he was expecting," they said. "He has been waiting for a gentleman for two days."

' "Where is he now?" I asked.

' "He is upstairs in bed. He wished to be called at nine."

' "I will go up and see him at once," I said.

'It seemed to me that my sudden appearance might shake his nerves[12] and lead him to say something unguarded[13]. The Boots[14] volunteered[15] to show me the room: it was on the second floor, and there was a small corridor leading up to it. The

1. le 3 au soir
2. les avertissant qu'il faudrait surveiller
3. les environs
4. je me disais
5. le plus naturel
6. de se loger
7. de rester aux environs de la gare
8. un lieu de rendez-vous
9. au préalable
10. sans aucun résultat
11. Quand j'ai demandé si
12. le déstabiliser
13. d'irréfléchi
14. garçon d'étage [lequel cire les chaussures]
15. a proposé

Boots pointed out the door to me, and was about to go downstairs again when I saw something that made me feel sickish[1], in spite of my twenty years' experience. From under the door there curled[2] a little red ribbon of blood, which had meandered across the passage[3] and formed a little pool along the skirting[4] at the other side. I gave a cry, which brought the Boots back. He nearly fainted[5] when he saw it. The door was locked on the inside, but we put our shoulders to it, and knocked it in[6]. The window of the room was open, and beside the window, all huddled up[7], lay the body of a man in his nightdress. He was quite dead, and had been for some time, for his limbs[8] were rigid and cold. When we turned him over, the Boots recognized him at once as being the same gentleman who had engaged the room under the name of Joseph Stangerson. The cause of death was a deep stab[9] in the left side, which must have penetrated the heart. And now comes the strangest part of the affair. What do you suppose was above the murdered man?'

I felt a creeping of the flesh[10], and a presentiment of coming horror, even before Sherlock Holmes answered.

'The word RACHE, written in letters of blood,' he said.

'That was it,' said Lestrade, in an awe-struck voice[11]; and we were all silent for a while.

There was something so methodical and so incomprehensible about the deeds[12] of this unknown assassin, that it imparted[13] a fresh ghastliness[14] to his crimes. My nerves, which were steady enough[15] on the field of battle tingled as I thought of it[16].

1. m'a donné la nausée
2. se déroulait
3. serpenté sur toute la largeur du couloir
4. plinthe
5. a failli s'évanouir
6. l'avons enfoncée à coups d'épaule
7. recroquevillé en tas
8. membres
9. coup de poignard
10. un frisson me parcourir
11. d'une voix emplie d'effroi
12. actes
13. apportait
14. un regain d'horreur
15. plutôt solides
16. tremblaient à cette idée

'The man was seen,' continued Lestrade. 'A milk boy[1], passing on his way to the dairy[2], happened to walk down the lane which leads from the mews[3] at the back of the hotel. He noticed that a ladder, which usually lay there[4], was raised against one of the windows of the second floor, which was wide open. After passing, he looked back and saw a man descend the ladder. He came down so quietly and openly[5] that the boy imagined him to be some carpenter[6] or joiner[7] at work in the hotel. He took no particular notice of[8] him, beyond thinking in his own mind[9] that it was early for him to be at work. He has an impression that the man was tall, had a reddish face, and was dressed in a long, brownish coat. He must have stayed in the room some little time after the murder, for we found blood-stained water in the basin[10], where he had washed his hands, and marks on the sheets where he had deliberately wiped[11] his knife.'

I glanced at Holmes on hearing the description of the murderer, which tallied[12] so exactly with his own. There was, however, no trace of exultation[13] or satisfaction upon his face.

'Did you find nothing in the room which could furnish a clue to[14] the murderer?' he asked.

'Nothing. Stangerson had Drebber's purse[15] in his pocket, but it seems that this was usual, as he did all the paying. There was eighty odd pounds[16] in it, but nothing had been taken. Whatever the motives of these extraordinary crimes, robbery is certainly not one of them. There were no papers or memoranda[17] in the murdered man's pocket, except a single telegram, dated from Cleveland about a month ago, and containing the words, 'J. H. is

1. garçon laitier
2. laiterie
3. rue [correspondant à d'anciennes écuries]
4. habituellement couchée là
5. tranquillement et ouvertement
6. charpentier
7. menuisier
8. attention à
9. si ce n'est de se dire en son for intérieur
10. cuvette
11. essuyé
12. correspondait
13. jubilation
14. un indice sur
15. le portefeuille
16. environ 80 livres [sterling]
17. ni aucune note

in Europe.' There was no name appended[1] to this message.'

'And there was nothing else?' Holmes asked.

'Nothing of any importance. The man's novel[2], with which he had read himself to sleep[3] was lying upon the bed, and his pipe was on a chair beside him. There was a glass of water on the table, and on the window-sill[4] a small chip ointment box[5] containing a couple of pills.'

Sherlock Holmes sprang from his chair with an exclamation of delight.

'The last link[6],' he cried, exultantly. 'My case is complete[7].'

The two detectives stared at him in amazement.

'I have now in my hands,' my companion said, confidently[8], 'all the threads which have formed such a tangle[9]. There are, of course, details to be filled in[10], but I am as certain of all the main facts, from the time that Drebber parted from Stangerson at the station, up to[11] the discovery of the body of the latter, as if I had seen them with my own eyes. I will give you a proof of my knowledge. Could you lay your hand upon those pills?'

'I have them,' said Lestrade, producing a small white box; 'I took them and the purse and the telegram, intending to have them put in a place of safety[12] at the Police Station. It was the merest chance my taking these pills[13], for I am bound to say[14] that I do not attach any importance to them.'

'Give them here,' said Holmes. 'Now, Doctor,' turning to me, 'are those ordinary pills?'

They certainly were not. They were of a pearly grey[15] colour, small, round, and almost transparent against the light. 'From[16] their lightness and trans-

1. joint
2. roman
3. qu'il avait lu pour s'endormir
4. rebord de la fenêtre
5. boîte à onguent ouvragée
6. maillon
7. J'ai tous les éléments de l'affaire
8. avec assurance
9. les fils de l'écheveau qui était à démêler
10. à préciser
11. jusqu'à
12. dans l'intention de les mettre en sûreté
13. C'est le plus grand des hasards si j'ai pris ces pilules
14. car il faut bien dire
15. gris perle
16. Au vu de

parency, I should imagine that they are soluble in water,' I remarked.

'Precisely so,' answered Holmes. 'Now would you mind going down and fetching that poor little devil of a terrier[1] which has been bad[2] so long, and which[3] the landlady wanted you to put out of its pain[4] yesterday.'

I went downstairs and carried the dog upstairs in my arms. It's laboured[5] breathing and glazing[6] eye showed that it was not far from its end. Indeed, its snow-white muzzle[7] proclaimed[8] that it had already exceeded[9] the usual term of canine existence. I placed it upon a cushion on the rug.

'I will now cut one of these pills in two,' said Holmes, and drawing his penknife[10] he suited the action to the word[11]. 'One half we return into the box for future purposes. The other half I will place in this wine glass, in which is a teaspoonful of water. You perceive[12] that our friend, the Doctor, is right, and that it readily[13] dissolves.'

'This may be very interesting,' said Lestrade, in the injured[14] tone of one who suspects that he is being laughed at[15], 'I cannot see, however, what it has to do with the death of Mr. Joseph Stangerson.'

'Patience, my friend, patience! You will find in time[16] that it has everything to do with it[17]. I shall now add a little milk to make the mixture palatable[18], and on presenting it to the dog we find that he laps it[19] up readily enough.'

As he spoke he turned the contents of the wine glass into a saucer[20] and placed it in front of the terrier, who speedily licked it dry[21]. Sherlock Holmes' earnest demeanour[22] had so far convinced us that we all sat in silence, watching the animal intently[23], and expecting[24] some startling[25] effect. None

1. fox-terrier
2. mal en point
3. dont
4. vous voir mettre fin à ses souffrances
5. difficile
6. vitreux
7. museau
8. montrait bien
9. dépassé
10. canif
11. joignit le geste à la parole
12. constatez
13. rapidement
14. froissé
15. qu'on se moque de lui
16. le moment venu
17. les deux éléments sont très liés
18. agréable au goût
19. va le laper
20. soucoupe
21. en lécha tout le contenu
22. détermination
23. attentivement
24. nous attendant à
25. surprenant

1. Il n'en fut rien
2. d'avoir bu cette mixture
3. mâchouillait
4. tambourinait des doigts
5. arboraient un sourire narquois
6. échec
7. qu'il subissait
8. arpentant furieusement
9. précisément
10. sans effet
11. ne s'en porte pas plus mal
12. cri perçant
13. À peine le pauvre animal y eut-il trempé la langue
14. que chacun de ses membres fut pris d'une convulsion
15. la foudre
16. poussa un long soupir
17. être plus confiant
18. suite
19. il se révèle invariablement
20. à même d'être interpreté différemment

such appeared[1], however. The dog continued to lie stretched upon the cushion, breathing in a laboured way, but apparently neither the better nor the worse for its draught[2].

Holmes had taken out his watch, and as minute followed minute without result, an expression of the utmost chagrin and disappointment appeared upon his features. He gnawed[3] his lip, drummed his fingers[4] upon the table, and showed every other symptom of acute impatience. So great was his emotion, that I felt sincerely sorry for him, while the two detectives smiled derisively[5], by no means displeased at this check[6] which he had met[7].

'It can't be a coincidence,' he cried, at last springing from his chair and pacing wildly up and down[8] the room; 'it is impossible that it should be a mere coincidence. The very pills which I suspected in the case of Drebber are actually[9] found after the death of Stangerson. And yet they are inert[10]. What can it mean? Surely my whole chain of reasoning cannot have been false. It is impossible! And yet this wretched dog is none the worse[11]. Ah, I have it! I have it!' With a perfect shriek[12] of delight he rushed to the box, cut the other pill in two, dissolved it, added milk, and presented it to the terrier. The unfortunate creature's tongue seemed hardly to have been moistened in it[13] before it gave a convulsive shiver in every limb[14], and lay as rigid and lifeless as if it had been struck by lightning[15].

Sherlock Holmes drew a long breath[16], and wiped the perspiration from his forehead. 'I should have more faith[17],' he said; 'I ought to know by this time that when a fact appears to be opposed to a long train[18] of deductions, it invariably proves to be[19] capable of bearing some other interpretation[20]. Of the two pills in that box one was of the most deadly[1] poison, and the other was entirely harmless[2]. I ought to have known that before ever I saw the box at all.'

This last statement appeared to me to be so startling, that I could hardly believe that he was in his sober senses[3]. There was the dead dog, however, to prove that his conjecture[4] had been correct. It seemed to me that the mists in my own mind were gradually clearing away, and I began to have a dim, vague[5] perception of the truth.

'All this seems strange to you,' continued Holmes, 'because you failed at the beginning of the inquiry to grasp[6] the importance of the single real clue which was presented to you. I had the good fortune to seize upon that[7], and everything which has occurred since then has served to confirm my original[8] supposition, and, indeed[9], was the logical sequence of it[10]. Hence[11] things which have perplexed you and made the case more obscure, have served to enlighten me and to strengthen my conclusions. It is a mistake to confound strangeness with mystery[12]. The most commonplace[13] crime is often the most mysterious because it presents no new or special features[14] from which deductions may be drawn. This murder would have been infinitely more difficult to unravel[15] had the body of the victim been simply found lying in the roadway without any of those *outré* and sensational accompaniments[16] which have rendered it remarkable. These strange details, far from making the case more difficult, have really had the effect of making it less so.'

Mr. Gregson, who had listened to this address[17] with considerable impatience, could contain himself

1. assurément mortel
2. inoffensive
3. qu'il n'ait pas bu
4. hypothèse
5. très vague
6. saisir
7. de la déceler
8. de départ
9. à vrai dire
10. en était la suite logique
11. En conséquence,
12. l'insolite et le mystérieux
13. banal
14. caractéristiques
15. à élucider
16. éléments subsidiaires
17. discours

no longer. 'Look here[1], Mr. Sherlock Holmes,' he said, 'we are all ready to acknowledge[2] that you are a smart man, and that you have your own methods of working. We want something more than mere theory and preaching[3] now, though. It is a case of taking[4] the man. I have made my case out[5], and it seems I was wrong. Young Charpentier could not have been engaged in[6] this second affair. Lestrade went after his man, Stangerson, and it appears that he was wrong too. You have thrown out hints here[7], and hints there[8], and seem to know more than we do, but the time has come when we feel that we have a right to ask you straight how much you do know of the business. Can you name the man who did it?'

'I cannot help feeling that Gregson is right, sir,' remarked Lestrade. 'We have both tried, and we have both failed. You have remarked more than once since I have been in the room that you had all the evidence[9] which you require. Surely you will not withhold it[10] any longer.'

'Any delay[11] in arresting the assassin,' I observed, 'might give him time to perpetrate some fresh[12] atrocity.'

Thus pressed by us all, Holmes showed signs of irresolution[13]. He continued to walk up and down the room with his head sunk[14] on his chest and his brows drawn down, as was his habit when lost in thought.

'There will be no more murders,' he said at last, stopping abruptly and facing us. 'You can put that consideration out of the question. You have asked me if I know the name of the assassin. I do. The mere knowing of[15] his name is a small thing[16], however, compared with the power of laying our

1. Écoutez
2. reconnaître
3. que juste une théorie et un sermon
4. Il s'agit de mettre la main sur
5. donné ma vision de l'affaire
6. avoir pris part à
7. laissé entendre ceci
8. puis cela
9. les preuves
10. n'allez pas les garder pour vous
11. retard
12. nouvelle
13. parut indécis
14. baissée
15. simple fait de connaître
16. n'est rien

hands upon him[1]. This I expect very shortly to do. I have good hopes of managing it through my own arrangements[2]; but it is a thing which needs delicate handling[3], for we have a shrewd[4] and desperate[5] man to deal with, who is supported[6], as I have had occasion to prove, by another who is as clever as himself. As long as this man has no idea[7] that anyone can have a clue[8] there is some chance of securing him[9]; but if he had the slightest suspicion, he would change his name, and vanish in an instant among the four million inhabitants of this great city. Without meaning to hurt either of your feelings[10], I am bound to say that I consider these men to be more than a match[11] for the official force[12], and that is why I have not asked your assistance. If I fail[13] I shall, of course, incur[14] all the blame due to this omission[15]; but that I am prepared for. At present I am ready to promise that the instant that I can communicate with you without endangering my own combinations[16], I shall do so.'

Gregson and Lestrade seemed to be far from satisfied by this assurance, or by the depreciating[17] allusion to the detective police[18]. The former had flushed up to the roots of his flaxen[19] hair, while the other's beady[20] eyes glistened with curiosity and resentment[21]. Neither of them had time to speak, however, before there was a tap at the door, and the spokesman[22] of the street Arabs[23], young Wiggins, introduced his insignificant and unsavoury[24] person.

'Please, sir,' he said, touching his forelock[25], 'I have the cab downstairs.'

'Good boy,' said Holmes, blandly[26]. 'Why don't you introduce this pattern[27] at Scotland Yard?' he continued, taking a pair of steel handcuffs[28] from

1. nous emparer de lui
2. d'y parvenir à ma façon
3. cela exige du doigté
4. malin
5. prêt à tout
6. soutenu
7. ne se doute pas
8. que quelqu'un détient une piste,
9. mettre la main sur lui
10. vouloir vous froisser ni l'un ni l'autre
11. ces hommes représentent d'après moi un trop gros morceau
12. pour la police
13. j'échoue,
14. j'endosserai, bien sûr
15. résultant de cet échec
16. arrangements
17. peu élogieuse
18. police judiciaire
19. filasse
20. perçants
21. de rancune
22. porte-parole
23. gamins des rues
24. peu ragoûtante
25. en saluant d'un geste [portant la main à son front]
26. d'un ton placide
27. modèle
28. menottes

a drawer. 'See how beautifully the spring works[1]. They fasten[2] in an instant.'

'The old pattern is good enough,' remarked Lestrade, 'if we can only find the man to put them on.'

'Very good, very good,' said Holmes, smiling. 'The cabman may as well help me with my boxes[3]. Just ask him to step up, Wiggins.'

I was surprised to find[4] my companion speaking as though he were about to set out on a journey[5], since he had not said anything to me about it. There was a small portmanteau[6] in the room, and this he pulled out and began to strap[7]. He was busily engaged at it[8] when the cabman entered the room.

'Just give me a help with this buckle[9], cabman,' he said, kneeling over his task, and never turning his head.

The fellow came forward with a somewhat sullen[10], defiant[11] air, and put down his hands to assist. At that instant there was a sharp click, the jangling of metal[12], and Sherlock Holmes sprang to his feet again.

'Gentlemen,' he cried, with flashing eyes, 'let me introduce you to Mr. Jefferson Hope, the murderer of Enoch Drebber and of Joseph Stangerson.'

The whole thing occurred in a moment — so quickly that I had no time to realize it. I have a vivid recollection[13] of that instant, of Holmes' triumphant expression and the ring[14] of his voice, of the cabman's dazed[15], savage face, as he glared at the glittering[16] handcuffs, which had appeared as if by magic upon his wrists. For a second or two we might have been a group of statues. Then, with an inarticulate roar of fury, the prisoner wrenched

1. comme le ressort fonctionne bien
2. se referment
3. bagages
4. d'entendre
5. partir en voyage
6. valise
7. à en attacher les sangles
8. s'y employait activement
9. boucle
10. renfrogné
11. méfiant
12. un bruit métallique
13. vif souvenir
14. timbre
15. hébété
16. étincelantes

himself free from[1] Holmes's grasp[2], and hurled himself[3] through the window. Woodwork[4] and glass gave way[5] before him; but before he got quite through, Gregson, Lestrade, and Holmes sprang upon him like so many staghounds[6]. He was dragged back into the room, and then commenced a terrific conflict. So powerful and so fierce[7] was he, that the four of us were shaken off again and again[8]. He appeared to have the convulsive strength of a man in an epileptic fit[9]. His face and hands were terribly mangled[10] by his passage through the glass, but loss of blood had no effect in diminishing his resistance. It was not until Lestrade succeeded in getting his hand inside his neckcloth[11] and half-strangling him that we made him realize that his struggles were of no avail[12]; and even then we felt no security until we had pinioned[13] his feet as well as his hands. That done, we rose to our feet breathless and panting[14].

'We have his cab,' said Sherlock Holmes. 'It will serve to take him to Scotland Yard. And now, gentlemen,' he continued, with a pleasant smile, 'we have reached the end of our little mystery. You are very welcome to put any questions that you like to me now, and there is no danger that I will refuse to answer them.'

1. s'arracha à
2. l'étreinte
3. se rua
4. La boiserie
5. cédèrent
6. autant de chiens de chasse
7. acharné
8. qu'il ne cessait de nous repousser tous les quatre
9. en pleine crise d'épilepsie
10. mutilés
11. cravate
12. ses efforts étaient voués à l'échec
13. avant d'avoir entravé
14. à bout de souffle

PART II

The Country of the Saints

CHAPTER I

On the Great Alkali[1] Plain

IN the central portion of the great North American Continent there lies[2] an arid and repulsive desert, which for many a long year served as a barrier against the advance of civilisation. From the Sierra Nevada to Nebraska, and from the Yellowstone River in the north to the Colorado upon the south, is a region of desolation and silence. Nor is Nature always in one mood[3] throughout this grim district[4]. It comprises[5] snow-capped and lofty[6] mountains, and dark and gloomy valleys. There are swift-flowing rivers which dash through jagged[7] cañons; and there are enormous plains, which in winter are white with snow, and in summer are grey with the saline alkali dust. They all preserve[8], however, the common characteristics of barrenness[9], inhospitality, and misery[10].

There are no inhabitants of this land of despair. A band of Pawnees or of Blackfeet may occasionally traverse it in order to reach other hunting-grounds, but the hardiest of the braves are glad to lose sight of those awesome[11] plains, and to find themselves once more upon their prairies. The coyote skulks[12] among the scrub[13], the buzzard[14] flaps heavily through the air[15], and the clumsy[16] grizzly bear lumbers[17] through the dark ravines, and picks

1. salée
2. s'étend
3. Mais la nature peut être d'humeur changeante
4. sur tout ce morne territoire
5. On y trouve
6. de hautes
7. accidentés
8. conservent
9. l'aridité
10. la désolation
11. menaçantes
12. rôde
13. fourrés
14. vautour
15. vole lourdement dans les airs
16. balourd
17. avance pesamment

up such sustenance as it can[1] amongst the rocks. These are the sole dwellers in the wilderness[2].

In the whole world there can be no more dreary view than[3] that from[4] the northern slope[5] of the Sierra Blanco. As far as the eye can reach stretches the great flat plain-land, all dusted over with patches of alkali, and intersected[6] by clumps of the dwarfish chaparral bushes[7]. On the extreme verge[8] of the horizon lie a long chain of mountain peaks, with their rugged summits flecked with[9] snow. In this great stretch of country there is no sign of life, nor of anything appertaining to life. There is no bird in the steel-blue heaven, no movement upon the dull, grey earth — above all, there is absolute silence. Listen as one may, there is no shadow of a sound in all that mighty wilderness; nothing but silence — complete and heart-subduing[10] silence.

It has been said there is nothing appertaining to life upon the broad plain. That is hardly true. Looking down from the Sierra Blanco, one sees a pathway traced out across the desert, which winds away and is lost in the extreme distance[11]. It is rutted with wheels[12] and trodden down by the feet of many adventurers[13]. Here and there there are scattered white objects which glisten in the sun, and stand out against[14] the dull deposit of alkali. Approach, and examine them! They are bones: some large and coarse, others smaller and more delicate. The former have belonged to oxen, and the latter to men. For fifteen hundred miles[15] one may trace[16] this ghastly caravan route[17] by these scattered remains of those who had fallen by the wayside.

Looking down on this very scene[18], there stood upon the fourth of May, eighteen hundred and forty-seven, a solitary traveller. His appearance

1. le peu de nourriture qu'il peut trouver
2. ces contrées sauvages
3. de paysage plus désolé que
4. celui que l'on voit depuis
5. versant
6. parsemé
7. des buissons nains du chaparral [sorte de garrigue]
8. Aux confins
9. tachetés de
10. oppressant
11. qui serpente pour se perdre dans les lointains
12. Des roues y ont creusé des ornières
13. bien des aventuriers y ont laissé les traces de leurs pas
14. se détachent sur
15. Sur 2 400 km,
16. il est possible de suivre
17. effrayante route caravanière
18. Contemplant précisément ce décor

was such that he might have been the very genius or demon of the region. An observer would have found it difficult to say whether he was nearer to forty or to sixty. His face was lean[1] and haggard[2], and the brown parchment-like[3] skin was drawn tightly[4] over the projecting[5] bones; his long, brown hair and beard were all flecked[6] and dashed with[7] white; his eyes were sunken in his head, and burned with an unnatural lustre; while the hand which grasped his rifle was hardly more fleshy[8] than that of a skeleton. As he stood, he leaned upon his weapon for support, and yet his tall figure and the massive framework[9] of his bones suggested a wiry[10] and vigorous constitution. His gaunt[11] face, however, and his clothes, which hung so baggily[12] over his shrivelled limbs[13], proclaimed what it was that gave him that senile and decrepit appearance. The man was dying — dying from hunger and from thirst.

He had toiled painfully down the ravine[14], and on to this little elevation[15], in the vain hope of seeing some signs of water. Now the great salt plain stretched before his eyes, and the distant belt of savage mountains, without a sign anywhere of plant or tree, which might indicate the presence of moisture. In all that broad landscape there was no gleam[16] of hope. North, and east, and west he looked with wild questioning eyes[17], and then he realised that his wanderings[18] had come to an end, and that there, on that barren[19] crag[20], he was about to die. 'Why not here, as well as in a feather bed, twenty years hence[21],' he muttered, as he seated himself in the shelter of a boulder[22].

Before sitting down, he had deposited upon the ground his useless rifle, and also a large

1. émacié
2. hâve
3. parcheminée
4. tendue à l'extrême
5. saillants
6. piquetés
7. mouchetés de
8. charnue
9. charpente
10. robuste
11. décharné
12. bien trop flottants
13. membres décharnés
14. péniblement suivi la pente du ravin
15. puis avait gravi ce monticule
16. lueur
17. l'œil farouche, scrutateur
18. errance
19. nu
20. escarpement rocheux
21. dans vingt ans
22. à l'abri d'un rocher

bundle[1] tied up in a grey shawl, which he had carried slung[2] over his right shoulder. It appeared to be somewhat too heavy for his strength, for[3] in lowering it, it came down on the ground with some little violence. Instantly there broke[4] from the grey parcel a little moaning[5] cry, and from it there protruded[6] a small, scared face, with very bright brown eyes, and two little speckled[7], dimpled[8] fists.

'You've hurt me!' said a childish voice reproachfully.

'Have I though[9],' the man answered penitently[10], 'I didn't go for to do it[11].' As he spoke he unwrapped the grey shawl and extricated[12] a pretty little girl of about five years of age, whose dainty[13] shoes and smart pink frock[14] with its little linen apron all bespoke[15] a mother's care[16]. The child was pale and wan[17], but her healthy arms and legs showed that she had suffered less than her companion.

'How is it now?' he answered anxiously, for she was still rubbing the towsy[18] golden curls which covered the back of her head.

'Kiss it and make it well,' she said, with perfect gravity, showing the injured part up to him. 'That's what mother used to do. Where's mother?'

'Mother's gone. I guess you'll see her before long.'

'Gone, eh!' said the little girl. 'Funny, she didn't say good-bye; she 'most[19] always did if she was just goin' over to Auntie's for tea, and now she's been away three days. Say, it's awful dry, ain't it? Ain't there no water, nor nothing to eat?'

'No, there ain't nothing, dearie. You'll just need to be patient awhile, and then you'll be all right. Put your head up agin[20] me like that, and then you'll feel bullier[21]. It ain't easy to talk when your

1. paquet
2. en bandoulière
3. car
4. s'échappa
5. plaintif
6. il en sortit
7. couverts de taches de rousseur
8. potelés
9. Ah bon ?
10. regretta l'homme
11. ne l'ai pas fait exprès
12. en sortit
13. jolis
14. robe
15. témoignaient des
16. soins attentionnés d'une mère
17. blême
18. ébouriffées
19. [almost]
20. [= against]
21. beaucoup mieux

lips is like leather, but I guess[1] I'd best let you know[2] how the cards lie[3]. What's that you've got?'

'Pretty things! fine things!' cried the little girl enthusiastically, holding up two glittering fragments of mica. 'When we goes back to home I'll give them to brother Bob.'

'You'll see prettier things than them soon,' said the man confidently[4]. 'You just wait a bit. I was going to tell you though — you remember when we left the river?'

'Oh, yes.'

'Well, we reckoned we'd strike[5] another river soon, d'ye see. But there was somethin' wrong; compasses[6], or map, or somethin', and it didn't turn up[7]. Water ran out[8]. Just except a little drop for the likes of you[9] and — and —'

'And you couldn't wash yourself,' interrupted his companion gravely, staring up at his grimy[10] visage.

'No, nor drink. And Mr. Bender, he was the fust[11] to go, and then Indian Pete, and then Mrs. McGregor, and then Johnny Hones, and then, dearie, your mother.'

'Then mother's a deader[12] too,' cried the little girl dropping her face in her pinafore[13] and sobbing bitterly[14].

'Yes, they all went except you and me. Then I thought there was some chance of water in this direction, so I heaved you[15] over my shoulder and we tramped it[16] together. It don't seem as though we've improved matters[17]. There's an almighty small chance for us[18] now!'

'Do you mean that we are going to die too?' asked the child, checking her sobs[19], and raising her tear-stained face.

1. suppose
2. que je ferais mieux de te dire
3. dans quelle situation nous nous trouvons
4. d'un ton assuré
5. on pensait qu'on tomberait sur
6. les boussoles
7. on ne l'a pas trouvée
8. On n'avait plus d'eau
9. toi
10. crasseux
11. [first]
12. [dead]
13. tablier
14. en pleurant à chaudes larmes
15. t'ai hissée
16. et nous sommes partis
17. La situation ne semble pas s'être améliorée
18. Nos chances sont très minces
19. contenant ses pleurs

'I guess that's about the size of it[1].'

'Why didn't you say so before?' she said, laughing gleefully[2]. 'You gave me such a fright. Why, of course, now as long as we die we'll be with mother again.'

'Yes, you will, dearie.'

'And you too. I'll tell her how awful good you've been. I'll bet she meets us at the door of Heaven with a big pitcher[3] of water, and a lot of buckwheat cakes[4], hot, and toasted on both sides, like Bob and me was fond of. How long will it be first?'

'I don't know — not very long.' The man's eyes were fixed upon the northern horizon. In the blue vault[5] of the heaven there had appeared three little specks[6] which increased in size every moment, so rapidly did they approach. They speedily resolved themselves into[7] three large brown birds, which circled over the heads of the two wanderers[8], and then settled upon some rocks which overlooked them[9]. They were buzzards, the vultures of the west, whose coming is the forerunner[10] of death.

'Cocks and hens,' cried the little girl gleefully, pointing at their ill-omened[11] forms, and clapping her hands to make them rise. 'Say, did God make this country?'

'Of course He did,' said her companion, rather startled by this unexpected question.

'He made the country down[12] in Illinois, and He made the Missouri,' the little girl continued. 'I guess somebody else made the country in these parts[13]. It's not nearly so well done. They forgot the water and the trees.'

'What would ye think of offering up prayer[14]?' the man asked diffidently[15].

'It ain't[16] night yet,' she answered.

1. oui, c'est à peu près ça
2. gaiement
3. cruche
4. [grosses] crêpes de sarrasin
5. voûte
6. points
7. prirent bientôt la forme de
8. voyageurs [errants]
9. qui les surplombaient
10. annonciatrice
11. de mauvais augure
12. là-bas
13. d'ici
14. de dire une prière
15. d'un ton mal assuré
16. [isn't]

'It don't matter. It ain't quite regular[1], but He won't mind that, you bet[2]. You say over them ones[3] that you used to say every night in the waggon when we was on the Plains.'

'Why don't you say some yourself?' the child asked, with wondering eyes[4].

'I disremember them[5],' he answered. 'I hain't said none since I was half the height o' that gun. I guess it's never too late. You say them out, and I'll stand by and come in on the choruses[6].'

'Then you'll need to kneel down, and me too,' she said, laying the shawl out for that purpose. 'You've got to put your hands up like this. It makes you feel kind o' good.'

It was a strange sight had there been anything but the buzzards[7] to see it. Side by side on the narrow shawl knelt the two wanderers, the little prattling child[8] and the reckless[9], hardened adventurer. Her chubby[10] face, and his haggard, angular visage were both turned up to the cloudless heaven in heartfelt entreaty[11] to that dread being[12] with whom they were face to face, while the two voices — the one thin and clear, the other deep and harsh — united in the entreaty for mercy[13] and forgiveness. The prayer finished, they resumed[14] their seat in the shadow of the boulder until the child fell asleep, nestling upon[15] the broad breast of her protector. He watched over her slumber[16] for some time, but Nature proved to be too strong for him. For three days and three nights hc had allowed himself neither rest nor repose[17]. Slowly the eyelids drooped[18] over the tired eyes, and the head sunk lower and lower upon the breast, until the man's grizzled beard was mixed with the gold

1. C'est pas tout à fait dans les règles
2. Il ne t'en voudra pas, j'en suis sûr
3. celles
4. l'air étonné
5. ne m'en souviens plus
6. répons
7. si les vautours n'avaient pas été les seuls
8. petite fille babillante
9. intrépide
10. joufflu
11. fervente prière
12. cet être redoutable
13. leur demande de miséricorde
14. reprirent
15. blottie contre
16. sommeil
17. aucun repos
18. s'affaissèrent

tresses[1] of his companion, and both slept the same deep and dreamless slumber.

Had the wanderer remained awake for another half hour a strange sight would have met his eyes. Far away on the extreme verge of the alkali plain there rose up a little spray of dust[2], very slight at first, and hardly to be distinguished from the mists of the distance, but gradually growing higher and broader until it formed a solid[3], well-defined cloud. This cloud continued to increase in size until it became evident that it could only be raised by a great multitude of moving creatures. In more fertile spots the observer would have come to the conclusion that one of those great herds of bisons which graze upon the prairie land was approaching him. This was obviously impossible in these arid wilds[4]. As the whirl[5] of dust drew nearer to the solitary bluff[6] upon which the two castaways[7] were reposing, the canvas-covered tilts of waggons[8] and the figures[9] of armed horsemen began to show up through the haze[10], and the apparition revealed itself as being a great caravan upon its journey for the West. But what a caravan! When the head of it had reached the base of the mountains, the rear[11] was not yet visible on the horizon. Right across the enormous plain stretched the straggling array,[12] waggons and carts, men on horseback, and men on foot. Innumerable women who staggered along under burdens[13], and children who toddled[14] beside the waggons or peeped out[15] from under the white coverings. This was evidently no ordinary party[16] of immigrants, but rather some nomad people who had been compelled[17] from stress of circumstances[18] to seek themselves a new country. There rose through the clear air a confused

1. boucles
2. nuée de poussière
3. massif
4. terres sauvages et arides
5. tourbillon
6. promontoire
7. proscrits
8. des chariots bâchés
9. silhouettes
10. brume
11. l'arrière
12. déploiement désordonné de
13. fardeaux
14. trottinaient
15. pointaient leur nez
16. troupe
17. forcé
18. par d'impérieuses circonstances

clattering[1] and rumbling[2] from this great mass of humanity, with the creaking of wheels and the neighing[3] of horses. Loud as it was[4], it was not sufficient to rouse[5] the two tired wayfarers[6] above them.

At the head of the column there rode a score[7] or more of grave ironfaced[8] men, clad in sombre homespun[9] garments[10] and armed with rifles. On reaching the base of the bluff they halted, and held a short council among themselves.

'The wells[11] are to the right, my brothers,' said one, a hard-lipped, clean-shaven man with grizzly hair.

'To the right of the Sierra Blanco — so we shall reach the Rio Grande,' said another.

'Fear not for water,' cried a third. 'He who could draw it[12] from the rocks will not now abandon His own chosen people[13].'

'Amen! Amen!' responded the whole party.

They were about to resume their journey[14] when one of the youngest and keenest-eyed[15] uttered[16] an exclamation and pointed up at the rugged crag above them. From its summit there fluttered[17] a little wisp of pink[18], showing up hard and bright against the grey rocks behind. At the sight there was a general reining up of horses and unslinging of guns[19], while fresh horsemen came galloping up to reinforce the vanguard[20]. The word 'Redskins' was on every lip.

'There can't be any number of Injuns[21] here,' said the elderly[22] man who appeared to be in command. 'We have passed the Pawnees, and there are no other tribes until we cross the great mountains.'

'Shall I go forward and see, Brother Stangerson,' asked one of the band.

'And I,' 'and I,' cried a dozen voices.

1. cliquetis
2. tohu-bohu
3. hennissement
4. Aussi fort que fût ce tintamarre
5. éveiller
6. voyageurs
7. vingtaine
8. inflexibles
9. tissés à la main
10. vêtements
11. sources
12. Celui qui a su la faire jaillir
13. Son peuple élu
14. reprendre leur route
15. au regard perçant
16. poussa
17. voletait
18. bout de tissu rose
19. Sur quoi chacun arrêta son cheval et tint son fusil prêt
20. avant-garde
21. Il ne peut pas y avoir beaucoup d'Indiens
22. vieil

'Leave your horses below and we will await you here,' the Elder answered. In a moment the young fellows had dismounted[1], fastened their horses, and were ascending the precipitous[2] slope which led up to the object which had excited their curiosity. They advanced rapidly and noiselessly, with the confidence[3] and dexterity of practised[4] scouts[5]. The watchers from the plain below could see them flit[6] from rock to rock until their figures stood out against the skyline[7]. The young man who had first given the alarm was leading them. Suddenly his followers saw him throw up his hands, as though overcome with astonishment, and on joining him they were affected[8] in the same way by the sight which met their eyes.

On the little plateau which crowned[9] the barren hill there stood a single giant boulder, and against this boulder there lay a tall man, long-bearded and hard-featured, but of an excessive thinness. His placid face and regular breathing showed that he was fast asleep[10]. Beside him lay a little child, with her round white arms encircling his brown sinewy[11] neck, and her golden haired head resting upon the breast of his velveteen[12] tunic. Her rosy lips were parted[13], showing the regular line of snow-white teeth within, and a playful[14] smile played over her infantile features. Her plump[15] little white legs terminating in white socks and neat shoes with shining buckles, offered a strange contrast to the long shrivelled[16] members of her companion. On the ledge of rock[17] above this strange couple there stood three solemn buzzards, who, at the sight of the newcomers uttered raucous screams of disappointment and flapped sullenly away[18].

1. mis pied à terre
2. escarpée
3. assurance
4. entraînés
5. éclaireurs
6. bondir
7. se découpent sur le ciel
8. réagirent
9. coiffait
10. dormait profondément
11. musclé
12. en velours de coton
13. entrouvertes
14. enjoué
15. dodues
16. desséchés
17. corniche rocheuse
18. s'envolèrent de mauvaise grâce

The cries of the foul birds[1] awoke the two sleepers who stared about them in bewilderment[2]. The man staggered to his feet[3] and looked down upon the plain which had been so desolate when sleep had overtaken him, and which was now traversed by this enormous body[4] of men and of beasts. His face assumed an expression of incredulity as he gazed, and he passed his boney[5] hand over his eyes. 'This is what they call delirium, I guess,' he muttered. The child stood beside him, holding on to the skirt[6] of his coat, and said nothing but looked all round her with the wondering questioning gaze of childhood.

The rescuing party[7] were speedily able to convince the two castaways that their appearance was no delusion[8]. One of them seized the little girl, and hoisted her upon his shoulder, while two others supported her gaunt companion, and assisted him towards the waggons.

'My name is John Ferrier,' the wanderer explained; 'me and that little un[9] are all that's left o' twenty-one people. The rest is all dead o' thirst and hunger away down in the south.'

'Is she your child?' asked someone.

'I guess she is now,' the other cried, defiantly[10]; 'she's mine 'cause I saved her. No man will take her from me. She's Lucy Ferrier from this day on[11]. Who are you, though?' he continued, glancing with curiosity at his stalwart[12], sunburned rescuers; 'there seems to be a powerful lot of ye[13].'

'Nigh upon[14] ten thousand,' said one of the young men; 'we are the persecuted children of God — the chosen of the Angel Merona.'

'I never heard tell on him[15],' said the wanderer. 'He appears to have chosen a fair crowd of ye[16].'

1. odieux volatiles
2. avec stupeur
3. se leva en titubant
4. foule
5. osseuse
6. le pan
7. sauveurs
8. une hallucination
9. [one]
10. d'un air de défi
11. dorénavant
12. robustes
13. vous paraissez bigrement nombreux
14. Pas loin de
15. [of him]
16. semble avoir choisi un bon paquet d'élus

1. Ne plaisantez pas avec le sacré
2. sévèrement
3. des plaques d'or martelé
4. loin des hommes violents et des impies
5. rafraîchit manifestement la mémoire de
6. par l'intermédiaire
7. pèlerins
8. dociles
9. au regard grave et tendu
10. compassion
11. dénuement
12. attirait le regard par
13. son élégance très voyante
14. y étaient attelés
15. tandis que les autres chariots n'en comptaient que deux ou, quatre, tout au plus.
16. le désignaient

'Do not jest at that which is sacred[1],' said the other sternly[2]. 'We are of those who believe in those sacred writings, drawn in Egyptian letters on plates of beaten gold[3], which were handed unto the holy Joseph Smith at Palmyra. We have come from Nauvoo, in the State of Illinois, where we had founded our temple. We have come to seek a refuge from the violent man and from the godless[4], even though it be the heart of the desert.'

The name of Nauvoo evidently recalled recollections to[5] John Ferrier. 'I see,' he said, 'you are the Mormons.'

'We are the Mormons,' answered his companions with one voice.

'And where are you going?'

'We do not know. The hand of God is leading us under the person[6] of our Prophet. You must come before him. He shall say what is to be done with you.'

They had reached the base of the hill by this time, and were surrounded by crowds of the pilgrims[7] — pale-faced meek-looking[8] women, strong laughing children, and anxious earnest-eyed[9] men. Many were the cries of astonishment and of commiseration[10] which arose from them when they perceived the youth of one of the strangers and the destitution[11] of the other. Their escort did not halt, however, but pushed on, followed by a great crowd of Mormons, until they reached a waggon, which was conspicuous for[12] its great size and for the gaudiness and smartness of its appearance[13]. Six horses were yoked to it[14], whereas the others were furnished with two, or, at most, four a-piece[15]. Beside the driver there sat a man who could not have been more than thirty years of age, but whose massive head and resolute expression marked him[16] as a leader. He was reading a brown-backed volume, but as the crowd approached he laid it aside, and listened attentively to an account[1] of the episode. Then he turned to the two castaways.

'If we take you with us,' he said, in solemn words, 'it can only be as believers in our own creed[2]. We shall have no wolves in our fold[3]. Better far[4] that your bones should bleach[5] in this wilderness than that you should prove to be[6] that little speck of decay[7] which in time corrupts the whole fruit. Will you come with us on these terms[8]?'

'Guess I'll come with you on any terms,' said Ferrier, with such emphasis that the grave Elders[9] could not restrain[10] a smile. The leader alone retained[11] his stern, impressive expression.

'Take him, Brother Stangerson,' he said, 'give him food and drink, and the child likewise. Let it be your task also to teach him our holy creed. We have delayed long enough[12]. Forward! On, on to Zion[13]!'

'On, on to Zion!' cried the crowd of Mormons, and the words rippled down the long caravan[14], passing from mouth to mouth until they died away in a dull murmur in the far distance. With a cracking of whips and a creaking of wheels the great waggons got into motion[15], and soon the whole caravan was winding along once more[16]. The Elder to whose care[17] the two waifs[18] had been committed[19], led them to his waggon, where a meal was already awaiting them.

'You shall remain here,' he said. 'In a few days you will have recovered from your fatigues. In the meantime, remember that now and for ever you are of our religion. Brigham Young[20] has said it, and he has spoken with the voice of Joseph Smith, which is the voice of God.'

1. compte rendu
2. croyance
3. bergerie
4. Il est bien préférable
5. blanchissent
6. plutôt que vous vous révéliez être
7. tache de pourriture
8. à cette condition
9. Anciens
10. ne purent réprimer
11. garda
12. nous sommes suffisamment attardés
13. Allons, en route vers Sion
14. parcoururent l'immense caravane
15. s'ébranlèrent
16. avait repris sa sinueuse progression
17. aux bons soins duquel
18. malheureux
19. confiés
20. [le successeur de Joseph Smith à la tête des mormons]

CHAPTER II

The Flower of Utah

1. rendre hommage aux épreuves
2. havre de paix
3. s'étaient acharnés à aller de l'avant
4. sans pareille
5. obstacle
6. des plus braves
7. arpents de terre vierge
8. se révéla
9. avisé
10. des cartes
11. ébauchée
12. On coupa la terre en lopins
13. on les attribua
14. dut reprendre
15. son ouvrage
16. des places
17. apparurent

THIS is not the place to commemorate the trials[1] and privations endured by the immigrant Mormons before they came to their final haven[2]. From the shores of the Mississippi to the western slopes of the Rocky Mountains they had struggled on[3] with a constancy almost unparalleled[4] in history. The savage man, and the savage beast, hunger, thirst, fatigue, and disease — every impediment[5] which Nature could place in the way, had all been overcome with Anglo-Saxon tenacity. Yet the long journey and the accumulated terrors had shaken the hearts of the stoutest[6] among them. There was not one who did not sink upon his knees in heartfelt prayer when they saw the broad valley of Utah bathed in the sunlight beneath them, and learned from the lips of their leader that this was the promised land, and that these virgin acres[7] were to be theirs for evermore.

Young speedily proved himself to be[8] a skilful[9] administrator as well as a resolute chief. Maps were drawn and charts[10] prepared, in which the future city was sketched out[11]. All around farms were apportioned[12] and allotted[13] in proportion to the standing of each individual. The tradesman was put to[14] his trade and the artisan to his calling[15]. In the town streets and squares[16] sprang up[17], as if by magic. In the country there was draining and hedging[1], planting and clearing[2], until the next summer saw the whole country golden with the wheat crop[3]. Everything prospered in the strange settlement[4]. Above all, the great temple which they had erected in the centre of the city grew ever taller and larger. From the first blush of dawn[5] until the closing of the twilight[6], the clatter of the hammer[7] and the rasp of the saw[8] was never absent from the monument which the immigrants erected to Him who had led them safe through many dangers.

The two castaways, John Ferrier and the little girl who had shared his fortunes[9] and had been adopted as his daughter, accompanied the Mormons to the end of their great pilgrimage. Little Lucy Ferrier was borne along[10] pleasantly enough in Elder Stangerson's waggon, a retreat[11] which she shared with the Mormon's three wives and with his son, a headstrong[12] forward[13] boy of twelve. Having rallied[14], with the elasticity[15] of childhood, from the shock caused by her mother's death, she soon became a pet with the women[16], and reconciled herself to[17] this new life in her moving canvas-covered home[18]. In the meantime Ferrier having recovered from his privations, distinguished himself as a useful guide and an indefatigable hunter. So rapidly did he gain the esteem of his new companions, that when they reached the end of their wanderings[19], it was unanimously agreed that he should be provided with[20] as large and as fertile a tract of land[21] as any of the settlers[22], with the exception of Young himself, and of Stangerson, Kemball, Johnston, and Drebber, who were the four principal Elders.

1. on draina et on planta des haies
2. on sema et on déboisa
3. par le blé
4. colonie
5. lueurs de l'aube
6. tombée de la nuit
7. coups de marteau
8. le grincement de la scie
9. destin
10. avait fait le voyage
11. refuge
12. têtu
13. et effronté
14. S'étant remise
15. faculté d'adaptation
16. la protégée des femmes
17. s'accoutuma à
18. maison de toile itinérante
19. pérégrinations
20. pour qu'il lui soit attribué
21. un terrain
22. colons

On the farm thus acquired John Ferrier built himself a substantial[1] log-house[2], which received so many additions[3] in succeeding years that it grew into a roomy[4] villa. He was a man of a practical turn of mind[5], keen[6] in his dealings and skilful with[7] his hands. His iron constitution enabled him to work morning and evening at improving and tilling his lands[8]. Hence it came about that[9] his farm and all that belonged to him prospered exceedingly[10]. In three years he was better off[11] than his neighbours, in six he was well-to-do[12], in nine he was rich, and in twelve there were not half a dozen men in the whole of Salt Lake City who could compare with him. From the great inland[13] sea to the distant Wahsatch Mountains there was no name better known than that of John Ferrier.

There was one way and only one in which he offended the susceptibilities of his co-religionists. No argument or persuasion could ever induce him[14] to set up a female establishment[15] after the manner of his companions. He never gave reasons for this persistent refusal, but contented himself by resolutely and inflexibly adhering to his determination[16]. There were some who accused him of lukewarmness[17] in his adopted religion, and others who put it down to[18] greed of wealth[19] and reluctance to incur expense[20]. Others, again, spoke of some early love affair, and of a fair-haired girl who had pined away[21] on the shores of the Atlantic. Whatever the reason, Ferrier remained strictly celibate[22]. In every other respect he conformed to the religion of the young settlement, and gained the name of being an orthodox and straight-walking[23] man.

1. imposante
2. maison en rondins
3. extensions
4. spacieuse
5. avait l'esprit pratique
6. perspicace
7. adroit de
8. à la mise en valeur et au travail de ses terres
9. C'est pourquoi
10. grandement
11. plus riche
12. aisé
13. intérieure
14. le convaincre
15. de prendre plusieurs femmes
16. s'en tenir à sa décision
17. tiédeur
18. expliquaient ce choix par
19. l'appât du gain
20. la réticence à engager des frais
21. dépéri
22. célibataire
23. droit

Lucy Ferrier grew up within the log-house, and assisted[1] her adopted father in all his undertakings[2]. The keen[3] air of the mountains and the balsamic odour of the pine trees took the place of[4] nurse and mother to the young girl. As year succeeded to year she grew taller and stronger, her cheek more ruddy[5], and her step more elastic. Many a wayfarer[6] upon the high road which ran by[7] Ferrier's farm felt long-forgotten thoughts revive in their mind[8] as they watched her lithe girlish figure[9] tripping through[10] the wheatfields, or met her mounted upon her father's mustang, and managing it[11] with all the ease and grace of a true child of the West. So the bud[12] blossomed[13] into a flower, and the year which saw her father the richest of the farmers left her[14] as fair a specimen of American girlhood[15] as could be found in the whole Pacific slope[16].

It was not the father, however, who first discovered that the child had developed into the woman. It seldom is in such cases. That mysterious change is too subtle and too gradual to be measured by dates. Least of all does the maiden herself know it[17] until the tone of a voice or the touch of a hand sets her heart thrilling within her[18], and she learns, with a mixture of pride and of fear, that a new and a larger nature has awoken within her. There are few who cannot recall[19] that day and remember the one little incident which heralded[20] the dawn of a new life. In the case of Lucy Ferrier the occasion was serious enough in itself, apart from its future influence on her destiny and that of many besides.

It was a warm June morning, and the Latter Day Saints[21] were as busy as the bees whose hive[22] they have chosen for their emblem. In the fields and in the streets rose the same hum[23] of human

1. seconda
2. entreprises
3. vif
4. tinrent lieu de
5. plus rose
6. Bien des voyageurs
7. passait devant
8. leur revenir à l'esprit
9. souple silhouette de jeune fille
10. traverser d'un pas léger
11. le conduisant
12. bouton
13. s'épanouit
14. fit d'elle
15. une des plus jolies jeunes Américaines
16. qu'on pût trouver sur tout le versant pacifique du pays
17. La jeune fille elle-même est la dernière à s'en rendre compte,
18. fasse tressaillir son cœur
19. se rappeler
20. annonciateur de
21. Saints des Derniers Jours [= mormons]
22. la ruche
23. bourdonnement

industry[1]. Down the dusty high roads defiled long streams[2] of heavily-laden[3] mules, all heading[4] to the west, for the gold fever had broken out in California, and the Overland Route[5] lay through the City of the Elect. There, too, were droves[6] of sheep and bullocks[7] coming in from the outlying pasture lands, and trains[8] of tired immigrants, men and horses equally weary of their interminable journey. Through all this motley[9] assemblage, threading her way[10] with the skill of an accomplished rider, there galloped Lucy Ferrier, her fair face flushed with[11] the exercise and her long chestnut hair floating out behind her. She had a commission from her father in the City, and was dashing in[12] as she had done many a time before, with all the fearlessness[13] of youth, thinking only of her task and how it was to be performed. The travel-stained[14] adventurers gazed after her in astonishment, and even the unemotional[15] Indians, journeying in with their peltries[16], relaxed their accustomed stoicism as they marvelled at the beauty of the pale-faced maiden.

She had reached the outskirts of the city when she found the road blocked by a great drove of cattle, driven by a half-dozen wild-looking herdsmen from the plains. In her impatience she endeavoured[17] to pass this obstacle by pushing her horse into what appeared to be a gap[18]. Scarcely had she got fairly into it, however, before[19] the beasts closed in behind her, and she found herself completely imbedded in the moving stream of fierce-eyed, long-horned bullocks. Accustomed as she was to deal with cattle, she was not alarmed at her situation, but took advantage of[20] every opportunity to urge her horse on[21] in the hopes of pushing her way through the cavalcade. Unfortunately the horns of one of the creatures, either by accident

1. activité
2. files
3. lourdement chargées
4. en route
5. voie par la route
6. des troupeaux
7. des bœufs
8. des convois
9. hétéroclite
10. se frayant un chemin
11. empourpré par
12. elle s'y rendait à bride abattue
13. intrépidité
14. couverts de poussière
15. impassibles
16. fourrures
17. s'efforça
18. trouée
19. que
20. mit à profit
21. pour pousser son cheval de l'avant

or design[1], came in violent contact with the flank of the mustang, and excited it to madness. In an instant it reared up upon its hind legs[2] with a snort of rage[3], and pranced and tossed[4] in a way that would have unseated[5] any but a most skilful rider[6]. The situation was full of peril. Every plunge of the excited horse brought it against the horns again, and goaded it to fresh madness[7]. It was all that the girl could do to keep herself in the saddle[8], yet a slip would mean a terrible death under the hoofs of the unwieldy[9] and terrified animals. Unaccustomed to sudden emergencies, her head began to swim[10], and her grip upon the bridle[11] to relax. Choked[12] by the rising cloud of dust and by the steam from the struggling creatures, she might have abandoned her efforts in despair, but for a kindly voice[13] at her elbow which assured her of assistance[14]. At the same moment a sinewy brown hand caught the frightened horse by the curb[15], and forcing a way through the drove, soon brought her to the outskirts.

'You're not hurt, I hope, miss,' said her preserver[16], respectfully.

She looked up at his dark, fierce face, and laughed saucily[17]. 'I'm awful frightened,' she said, naïvely; 'whoever would have thought that Poncho would have been so scared by a lot of cows?'

'Thank God you kept your seat[18],' the other said earnestly[19]. He was a tall, savage-looking young fellow, mounted on a powerful roan[20] horse, and clad in the rough dress of a hunter, with a long rifle slung over his shoulders. 'I guess you are the daughter of John Ferrier,' he remarked,

'I saw you ride down from his house. When you see him, ask him if he remembers the Jefferson Hopes of St. Louis. If he's the same Ferrier, my father and he were pretty thick[21].'

1. délibérément

2. se cabra

3. s'ébrouant rageusement

4. caracolant et renâclant

5. désarçonné

6. un cavalier moins émérite

7. et le rendait encore plus fou

8. La jeune fille avait toutes les peines du monde à rester en selle

9. massifs

10. tourner

11. bride

12. Suffoquée

13. si une voix bienveillante

14. ne lui avait proposé de l'aide

15. bride

16. sauveteur

17. eut un rire effronté

18. êtes restée en selle

19. avec conviction

20. rouan

21. très liés

'Hadn't you better come and ask yourself?' she asked, demurely[1].

The young fellow seemed pleased at the suggestion, and his dark eyes sparkled with pleasure. 'I'll do so,' he said, 'we've been in the mountains for two months, and are not over and above in visiting condition[2]. He must take us as he finds us.'

'He has a good deal to thank you for, and so have I,' she answered, 'he's awful fond of me. If those cows had jumped on me he'd have never got over it.'

'Neither would I,' said her companion.

'You! Well, I don't see that it would make much matter to you, anyhow. You ain't even a friend of ours.'

The young hunter's dark face grew so gloomy over[3] this remark that Lucy Ferrier laughed aloud.

'There, I didn't mean that,' she said; 'of course, you are a friend now. You must come and see us. Now I must push along[4], or father won't trust me with his business any more. Good-bye!'

'Good-bye,' he answered, raising his broad sombrero, and bending over her little hand. She wheeled her mustang round[5], gave it a cut with her riding-whip[6], and darted away down[7] the broad road in a rolling cloud of dust.

Young Jefferson Hope rode on with his companions, gloomy and taciturn. He and they had been among the Nevada Mountains prospecting for silver, and were returning to Salt Lake City in the hope of raising capital enough to work some lodes[8] which they had discovered. He had been as keen as any of them upon the business[9] until this sudden incident had drawn his thoughts into another channel[10]. The sight of the fair young girl, as frank and wholesome[11] as the Sierra breezes, had stirred his volcanic,

1. modestement
2. vraiment pas présentables pour une visite
3. si sombre en entendant
4. y aller
5. fit pivoter son mustang
6. lui donna un coup de cravache
7. fila sur
8. filons
9. Comme les autres, il s'était impliqué à fond dans cette affaire
10. direction
11. saine

untamed[1] heart to its very depths. When she had vanished from his sight, he realized that a crisis had come in his life, and that neither silver speculations[2] nor any other questions could ever be of such importance to him as this new and all-absorbing one. The love which had sprung up in his heart was not the sudden, changeable fancy[3] of a boy, but rather the wild, fierce passion of a man of strong will[4] and imperious temper. He had been accustomed to succeed in all that he undertook. He swore in his heart that he would not fail in this if human effort and human perseverance could render him successful.

He called on[5] John Ferrier that night, and many times again, until his face was a familiar one at the farm-house. John, cooped up[6] in the valley, and absorbed in his work, had had little chance of learning the news of the outside world during the last twelve years. All this Jefferson Hope was able to tell him, and in a style which interested Lucy as well as her father. He had been a pioneer in California, and could narrate many a strange tale of fortunes made and fortunes lost in those wild, halcyon[7] days. He had been a scout[8] too, and a trapper, a silver explorer, and a ranchman. Wherever stirring[9] adventures were to be had, Jefferson Hope had been there in search of them.

He soon became a favourite with the old farmer, who spoke eloquently of his virtues. On such occasions, Lucy was silent, but her blushing cheek and her bright, happy eyes, showed only too clearly that her young heart was no longer her own[10]. Her honest father may not have observed these symptoms, but they were assuredly not thrown away upon[11] the man who had won her affections.

1. indompté

2. ni la recherche de mines d'argent

3. le caprice soudain, inconstant

4. volonté

5. rendit visite à

6. reclus

7. de frénésie et de bonheur

8. éclaireur

9. exaltantes

10. ne lui appartenait plus

11. n'avaient certainement pas échappé à

It was a summer evening when he came galloping down the road and pulled up at[1] the gate. She was at the doorway, and came down to meet him. He threw the bridle over the fence and strode up the pathway.

'I am off[2], Lucy,' he said, taking her two hands in his, and gazing tenderly down into her face; 'I won't ask you to come with me now, but will you be ready to come when I am here again?'

'And when will that be?' she asked, blushing and laughing.

'A couple of months at the outside[3]. I will come and claim you then[4], my darling. There's no one who can stand[5] between us.'

'And how about father?' she asked.

'He has given his consent, provided[6] we get these mines working all right[7]. I have no fear on that head[8].'

'Oh, well; of course, if you and father have arranged it all, there's no more to be said,' she whispered, with her cheek against his broad breast.

'Thank God!' he said, hoarsely[9], stooping and kissing her[10]. 'It is settled[11], then. The longer I stay, the harder it will be to go. They are waiting for me at the cañon. Good-bye, my own darling — good-bye. In two months you shall see me.'

He tore himself from her as he spoke, and, flinging himself upon his horse, galloped furiously away, never even looking round, as though afraid that his resolution[12] might fail him[13] if he took one glance at what he was leaving. She stood at the gate, gazing after him until he vanished from her sight. Then she walked back into the house, the happiest girl in all Utah.

1. s'arrêta devant
2. Je m'en vais
3. au maximum
4. alors demander ta main
5. s'interposer
6. si
7. arrivons à lancer l'exploitation des mines
8. à ce sujet
9. d'une voix rauque
10. et il se pencha pour l'embrasser
11. réglé
12. détermination
13. ne vienne à faiblir

CHAPTER III

John Ferrier Talks with the Prophet

THREE weeks had passed since Jefferson Hope and his comrades had departed from Salt Lake City. John Ferrier's heart was sore within him[1] when he thought of the young man's return, and of the impending loss[2] of his adopted child. Yet her bright and happy face reconciled him to the arrangement[3] more than any argument could have done. He had always determined[4], deep down in his resolute heart, that nothing would ever induce him[5] to allow his daughter to wed a Mormon. Such a marriage he regarded as no marriage at all, but as a shame and a disgrace. Whatever he might think of the Mormon doctrines, upon that one point he was inflexible. He had to seal his mouth on the subject[6], however, for to express an unorthodox opinion was a dangerous matter in those days in the Land of the Saints.

Yes, a dangerous matter — so dangerous that even the most saintly dared only whisper their religious opinions with bated breath[7], lest[8] something which fell from their lips might be misconstrued[9], and bring down a swift retribution[10] upon them. The victims of persecution had now turned persecutors on their own account, and persecutors of the most terrible description[11]. Not the Inquisition of Seville, nor the German

1. avait le cœur lourd
2. perte prochaine
3. lui faisait accepter cette perspective
4. s'était toujours fixé pour règle
5. l'amener
6. Il devait taire sa façon de voir
7. à mi-voix
8. de peur que
9. mal interprété
10. châtiment rapide
11. espèce

Vehmgericht[1], nor the Secret Societies of Italy, were ever able to put a more formidable[2] machinery in motion than that which cast a cloud[3] over the State of Utah.

Its invisibility, and the mystery which was attached to it, made this organization doubly terrible. It appeared to be omniscient and omnipotent, and yet was neither seen nor heard. The man who held out against[4] the Church vanished away, and none knew whither[5] he had gone or what had befallen him[6]. His wife and his children awaited him at home, but no father ever returned to tell them how he had fared at[7] the hands of his secret judges. A rash[8] word or a hasty[9] act was followed by annihilation, and yet none knew what the nature might be of this terrible power which was suspended over them. No wonder that[10] men went about in fear and trembling, and that even in the heart of the wilderness they dared not whisper the doubts which oppressed them.

At first this vague and terrible power was exercised only upon the recalcitrants who, having embraced the Mormon faith, wished afterwards to pervert or to abandon it[11]. Soon, however, it took a wider range[12]. The supply of adult women was running short[13], and polygamy without a female population on which to draw[14] was a barren[15] doctrine indeed. Strange rumours began to be bandied about[16] — rumours of murdered immigrants and rifled[17] camps in regions where Indians had never been seen. Fresh women appeared in the harems of the Elders — women who pined[18] and wept, and bore upon their faces the traces of an unextinguishable horror. Belated[19] wanderers upon the mountains spoke of gangs of

1. Sainte-Vehme
2. terrible
3. jeta une ombre
4. résistait à
5. où
6. ou quel avait été son sort
7. ce qui lui était advenu entre
8. imprudent
9. impulsif
10. Rien d'étonnant si
11. la déformer ou la quitter
12. élargit son champ d'action
13. Les femmes adultes venaient à manquer
14. sans un vivier de femmes où s'approvisionner
15. vide
16. à circuler
17. pillés
18. dépérissaient
19. Attardés

armed men, masked, stealthy[1], and noiseless, who flitted[2] by them in the darkness. These tales and rumours took substance and shape[3], and were corroborated and re-corroborated, until they resolved themselves into a definite name[4]. To this day[5], in the lonely ranches of the West, the name of the Danite Band, or the Avenging Angels, is a sinister and an ill-omened[6] one.

Fuller knowledge of the organization which produced such terrible results served to increase rather than to lessen the horror which it inspired in the minds of men. None knew who belonged to this ruthless[7] society. The names of the participators in the deeds of blood and violence done under the name of religion were kept profoundly secret. The very friend to whom you communicated your misgivings[8] as to the Prophet and his mission, might be one of those who would come forth at night with fire and sword to exact a terrible reparation[9]. Hence[10] every man feared his neighbour, and none spoke of the things which were nearest his heart.

One fine morning, John Ferrier was about to set out to his wheatfields, when he heard the click of the latch[11], and, looking through the window, saw a stout, sandy-haired, middle-aged man coming up the pathway. His heart leapt to his mouth[12], for this was none other than the great Brigham Young himself. Full of trepidation[13] — for he knew that such a visit boded him little good[14] — Ferrier ran to the door to greet the Mormon chief. The latter, however, received his salutations coldly, and followed him with a stern face into the sitting-room.

1. furtifs
2. se glissaient
3. se précisèrent
4. se matérialiser sous un nom précis
5. Aujourd'hui encore
6. de mauvais augure
7. impitoyable
8. doutes
9. exercer une terrible vengeance
10. En conséquence
11. bruit du loquet
12. Il sentit son cœur défaillir
13. appréhension
14. n'annonçait rien de bon

1. jetant un regard perçant au fermier
2. très bonne part
3. t'enrichir
4. n'avons posé qu'une
5. si j'en crois la rumeur
6. en signe de protestation
7. beaucoup [d'hommes] pouvaient mieux y prétendre
8. pour prendre soin de moi
9. est tenue en grande estime
10. gémit intérieurement
11. que je suis prêt à ne pas croire
12. serait promise à un gentil [= païen]
13. Ce ne sont certainement que vains racontars

'Brother Ferrier,' he said, taking a seat, and eyeing the farmer keenly[1] from under his light-coloured eyelashes, 'the true believers have been good friends to you. We picked you up when you were starving in the desert, we shared our food with you, led you safe to the Chosen Valley, gave you a goodly share[2] of land, and allowed you to wax rich[3] under our protection. Is not this so?'

'It is so,' answered John Ferrier.

'In return for all this we asked but one[4] condition: that was, that you should embrace the true faith, and conform in every way to its usages. This you promised to do, and this, if common report says truly[5], you have neglected.'

'And how have I neglected it?' asked Ferrier, throwing out his hands in expostulation[6]. 'Have I not given to the common fund? Have I not attended at the Temple? Have I not — ?'

'Where are your wives?' asked Young, looking round him. 'Call them in, that I may greet them.'

'It is true that I have not married,' Ferrier answered. 'But women were few, and there were many who had better claims than I[7]. I was not a lonely man: I had my daughter to attend to my wants[8].'

'It is of that daughter that I would speak to you,' said the leader of the Mormons. 'She has grown to be the flower of Utah, and has found favour[9] in the eyes of many who are high in the land.'

John Ferrier groaned internally[10].

'There are stories of her which I would fain disbelieve[11] — stories that she is sealed to some Gentile[12]. This must be the gossip of idle tongues[13].

What is the thirteenth rule in the code of the sainted Joseph Smith? 'Let every maiden of the true faith marry one of the elect; for if she wed a Gentile, she commits a grievous sin[1].' This being so, it is impossible that you, who profess the holy creed, should suffer[2] your daughter to violate it.'

John Ferrier made no answer, but he played nervously with his riding-whip.

'Upon this one point your whole faith shall be tested[3] — so it has been decided in the Sacred Council of Four. The girl is young, and we would not have her wed grey hairs[4], neither would we deprive her of all choice. We Elders have many heifers[5]*, but our children must also be provided[6]. Stangerson has a son, and Drebber has a son, and either of them would gladly welcome your daughter to their house. Let her choose between them. They are young and rich, and of the true faith. What say you to that?'

Ferrier remained silent for some little time with his brows knitted[7].

'You will give us time,' he said at last. 'My daughter is very young — she is scarce[8] of an age to marry.'

'She shall have a month to choose,' said Young, rising from his seat. 'At the end of that time she shall give her answer.'

He was passing through the door, when he turned, with flushed face and flashing eyes. 'It were better for you, John Ferrier,' he thundered[9], 'that you and she were now lying blanched skeletons upon the Sierra Blanco, than that you should put your weak wills against the orders of the Holy Four!'

1. grave péché
2. tu tolères
3. éprouvée
4. un vieux barbon
5. génisses
6. pourvus
7. les sourcils froncés
8. n'est guère
9. tonna-t-il

**Herbert C. Kemball, in one of his sermons, alludes to his hundred wives under this endearing[10] epithet.*

10. affectueuse

With a threatening gesture of his hand, he turned from the door, and Ferrier heard his heavy step scrunching along the shingly path[1].

He was still sitting with his elbows upon his knees, considering how he should broach the matter to[2] his daughter when a soft hand was laid upon his, and looking up, he saw her standing beside him. One glance at her pale, frightened face showed him that she had heard what had passed.

'I could not help it,' she said, in answer to his look. 'His voice rang through[3] the house. Oh, father, father, what shall we do?'

'Don't you scare yourself,' he answered, drawing her to him, and passing his broad, rough hand caressingly over her chestnut hair. 'We'll fix it up[4] somehow or another. You don't find your fancy kind o' lessening for this chap, do you[5]?'

A sob and a squeeze of his hand was her only[6] answer.

'No; of course not. I shouldn't care to hear you say you did[7]. He's a likely[8] lad, and he's a Christian, which is more than these folk here, in spite o' all their praying and preaching. There's a party[9] starting for Nevada to-morrow, and I'll manage to send him a message letting him know the hole[10] we are in. If I know anything o' that young man, he'll be back here with a speed that would whip electro-telegraphs[11].'

Lucy laughed through her tears at her father's description.

'When he comes, he will advise us for the best. But it is for you that I am frightened, dear.

One hears — one hears such dreadful stories about those who oppose the Prophet: something terrible always happens to them.'

1. écraser le gravier de l'allée
2. aborder la question avec
3. résonnait dans toute
4. trouverons une solution
5. Ton penchant pour ce gars n'a pas faibli, n'est-ce pas
6. seule
7. Je n'aimerais pas t'entendre dire le contraire
8. sympathique
9. groupe
10. pétrin
11. de retour ici plus vite que le télégraphe [électrique]

'But we haven't opposed him yet,' her father answered. 'It will be time to look out for squalls when we do[1]. We have a clear month[2] before us; at the end of that, I guess we had best shin out[3] of Utah.'

'Leave Utah!'

'That's about the size of it[4].'

'But the farm?'

'We will raise as much as we can in money, and let the rest go[5]. To tell the truth, Lucy, it isn't the first time I have thought of doing it. I don't care about knuckling under to any man[6], as these folk do to their darned[7] prophet. I'm a free-born American, and it's all new to me. Guess I'm too old to learn. If he comes browsing[8] about this farm, he might chance to run up against[9] a charge of buckshot[10] travelling in the opposite direction.'

'But they won't let us leave,' his daughter objected.

'Wait till Jefferson comes, and we'll soon manage that. In the meantime, don't you fret yourself[11], my dearie, and don't get your eyes swelled up, else[12] he'll be walking into me[13] when he sees you. There's nothing to be afeared about, and there's no danger at all.'

John Ferrier uttered these consoling remarks in a very confident[14] tone, but she could not help observing that he paid unusual care to the fastening of the doors[15] that night, and that he carefully cleaned and loaded[16] the rusty[17] old shotgun which hung upon the wall of his bedroom.

1. C'est quand nous l'aurons fait qu'il faudra veiller au grain

2. un mois entier

3. déguerpir

4. Ça se résume à peu près à ça

5. abandonnerons le reste

6. n'aime pas me soumettre à quiconque

7. fichu

8. S'il vient traîner

9. il se pourrait bien qu'il rencontre

10. une décharge de chevrotine

11. ne te fais pas de mauvais sang

12. sinon

13. il va encore m'empoisonner

14. assuré

15. vérifia la fermeture des portes avec un soin tout particulier

16. chargea

17. rouillé

CHAPTER IV

A Flight for Life

ON the morning which followed his interview with the Mormon Prophet, John Ferrier went in to Salt Lake City, and having found his acquaintance,[1] who was bound for[2] the Nevada Mountains, he entrusted him with[3] his message to Jefferson Hope. In it he told the young man of the imminent danger which threatened them, and how necessary it was that he should return. Having done thus[4] he felt easier in his mind[5], and returned home with a lighter heart.

As he approached his farm, he was surprised to see a horse hitched[6] to each of the posts of the gate. Still more surprised was he on entering to find two young men in possession of[7] his sitting-room. One, with a long pale face, was leaning back in the rocking-chair, with his feet cocked up[8] upon the stove. The other, a bull-necked youth with coarse bloated[9] features, was standing in front of the window with his hands in his pocket, whistling a popular hymn. Both of them nodded[10] to Ferrier as he entered, and the one in the rocking-chair commenced the conversation.

'Maybe you don't know us,' he said. 'This here is the son of Elder Drebber, and I'm Joseph Stangerson, who travelled with you in the desert when the

1. la personne de sa connaissance
2. se rendait dans
3. lui confia
4. Après quoi,
5. se sentit l'esprit plus tranquille
6. attaché
7. installés dans
8. posés
9. bouffis
10. firent un petit signe de la tête

Lord stretched out His hand and gathered you into the true fold[1].'

'As He will all the nations[2] in His own good time[3],' said the other in a nasal voice; 'He grindeth[4] slowly but exceeding small[5].'

John Ferrier bowed[6] coldly. He had guessed who his visitors were.

'We have come,' continued Stangerson, 'at the advice of our fathers to solicit the hand of your daughter for whichever of us may seem good to you and to her. As I have but[7] four wives and Brother Drebber here has seven, it appears to me that my claim is the stronger one[8].'

'Nay, nay, Brother Stangerson,' cried the other; 'the question is not how many wives we have, but how many we can keep[9]. My father has now given over his mills[10] to me, and I am the richer man.'

'But my prospects[11] are better,' said the other, warmly. 'When the Lord removes[12] my father, I shall have his tanning yard and his leather factory[13]. Then[14] I am your elder, and am higher in the Church.'

'It will be for the maiden to decide,' rejoined[15] young Drebber, smirking at his own reflection in the glass[16]. 'We will leave it all to her decision.'

During this dialogue, John Ferrier had stood fuming[17] in the doorway, hardly able to keep his riding-whip[18] from the backs of his two visitors.

'Look here[19],' he said at last, striding up to them[20], 'when my daughter summons you[21], you can come, but until then I don't want to see your faces again.'

The two young Mormons stared at him in amazement. In their eyes this competition between them

1. pour vous mener dans le giron de la véritable Église
2. Comme Il le fera pour toutes les nations
3. quand telle sera Sa volonté
4. moud
5. très finement
6. salua
7. Comme je n'ai que
8. cela me donne l'avantage pour prétendre à sa main
9. entretenir
10. fabriques
11. espérances [pécunaires]
12. rappellera à Lui
13. sa tannerie et sa fabrique de cuir me reviendront
14. De plus,
15. répliqua
16. se souriant à lui-même dans le miroir d'un air satisfait
17. furibond
18. cravache
19. Écoutez-moi bien
20. en avançant vers eux à grandes enjambées
21. vous convoquera

for the maiden's hand was the highest of honours both to her and her father.

'There are two ways out of the room,' cried Ferrier; 'there is the door, and there is the window. Which do you care to use?'

His brown face looked so savage, and his gaunt[1] hands so threatening, that his visitors sprang to their feet and beat a hurried retreat[2]. The old farmer followed them to the door.

'Let me know when you have settled which it is to be[3],' he said, sardonically.

'You shall smart for this[4]!' Stangerson cried, white with rage. 'You have defied the Prophet and the Council of Four. You shall rue it[5] to the end of your days.'

'The hand of the Lord shall be heavy upon you[6],' cried young Drebber; 'He will arise and smite you[7]!'

'Then I'll start the smiting,' exclaimed Ferrier furiously, and would have rushed upstairs for his gun had not Lucy seized him by the arm and restrained him[8]. Before he could escape from her, the clatter of horses' hoofs told him that they were beyond his reach[9].

'The young canting rascals[10]!' he exclaimed, wiping the perspiration from his forehead; 'I would sooner see you in your grave, my girl, than the wife of either of them.'

'And so should I, father,' she answered, with spirit[11]; 'but Jefferson will soon be here.'

'Yes. It will not be long before he comes. The sooner the better, for we do not know what their next move may be[12].'

It was, indeed, high time[13] that someone capable of giving advice and help should come to the aid of the sturdy[14] old farmer and his adopted

1. décharnées
2. battirent précipitamment en retraite
3. Prévenez-moi quand vous aurez choisi lequel des deux
4. Il vous en cuira
5. le regretterez
6. s'abattra sur vous
7. vous frappera
8. pour le retenir
9. hors d'atteinte
10. Jeunes vauriens hypocrites
11. feu
12. comment ils réagiront
13. grand temps
14. solide

daughter. In the whole history of the settlement there had never been such a case of rank disobedience[1] to the authority of the Elders. If minor errors were punished so sternly, what would be the fate of this arch rebel[2]. Ferrier knew that his wealth and position would be of no avail to him[3]. Others as well known and as rich as himself had been spirited away[4] before now, and their goods given over to the Church. He was a brave man, but he trembled at the vague, shadowy terrors which hung[5] over him. Any known[6] danger he could face[7] with a firm lip[8], but this suspense was unnerving[9]. He concealed his fears from his daughter, however, and affected to make light of the whole matter[10], though she, with the keen eye[11] of love, saw plainly that he was ill at ease.

He expected that he would receive some message or remonstrance from Young as to his conduct, and he was not mistaken, though it came in an unlooked-for[12] manner. Upon rising next morning he found, to his surprise, a small square of paper pinned on to the coverlet of his bed just over his chest. On it was printed, in bold straggling letters[13]:

TWENTY-NINE DAYS ARE GIVEN YOU
FOR AMENDMENT[14], AND THEN —

The dash[15] was more fear-inspiring[16] than any threat[17] could have been. How this warning[18] came into his room puzzled John Ferrier sorely[19], for his servants slept in an outhouse[20], and the doors and windows had all been secured. He crumpled the paper up[21] and said nothing to his daughter, but the incident struck a chill into his heart[22]. The twenty-nine days were evidently

1. franche insoumission
2. rebelle notoire
3. ne lui seraient d'aucun secours
4. avaient été enlevés
5. planaient
6. identifié
7. affronter
8. sans frémir
9. mettait ses nerfs à rude épreuve
10. de prendre les choses à la légère
11. regard perçant
12. inattendue
13. écrit, en caractères gras et irréguliers
14. pour t'amender
15. Le tiret
16. effrayant
17. menace
18. avertissement
19. rendait John Ferrier extrêmement perplexe
20. remise
21. chiffonna le papier
22. lui glaça le cœur

the balance[1] of the month which Young had promised. What strength or courage could avail against[2] an enemy armed with such mysterious powers? The hand which fastened that pin might have struck him to the heart, and he could never have known who had slain him.

Still more shaken was he next morning. They had sat down to their breakfast when Lucy with a cry of surprise pointed upwards. In the centre of the ceiling was scrawled[3], with a burned stick apparently, the number 28. To his daughter it was unintelligible, and he did not enlighten her[4]. That night he sat up with his gun and kept watch and ward[5]. He saw and he heard nothing, and yet in the morning a great 27 had been painted upon the outside of his door.

Thus day followed day; and as sure as morning came[6] he found that his unseen enemies had kept their register[7], and had marked up in some conspicuous position[8] how many days were still left to him out of the month of grace. Sometimes the fatal numbers appeared upon the walls, sometimes upon the floors, occasionally they were on small placards[9] stuck upon the garden gate or the railings[10]. With[11] all his vigilance John Ferrier could not discover whence[12] these daily warnings proceeded[13]. A horror which was almost superstitious came upon him at the sight of them. He became haggard and restless, and his eyes had the troubled[14] look of some hunted creature. He had but one hope in life[15] now, and that was for the arrival of the young hunter from Nevada.

Twenty had changed to fifteen and fifteen to ten, but there was no news of the absentee. One

1. ce qu'il restait
2. s'opposer à
3. griffonné
4. ne chercha pas à l'éclairer
5. monta la garde
6. aussi sûr que le soleil se levait chaque matin,
7. fait leur décompte
8. à un endroit bien en vue
9. des affichettes
10. grille
11. Malgré
12. d'où
13. provenaient
14. affolé
15. Un seul espoir lui restait

by one the numbers dwindled down[1], and still there came no sign of him. Whenever a horseman clattered down the road, or a driver shouted at his team[2], the old farmer hurried to the gate thinking that help had arrived at last. At last, when he saw five give way to four and that again to three, he lost heart[3], and abandoned all hope of escape. Single-handed[4], and with his limited knowledge of the mountains which surrounded the settlement, he knew that he was powerless. The more-frequented roads were strictly watched and guarded, and none could pass along them[5] without an order from the Council. Turn which way he would[6], there appeared to be no avoiding[7] the blow which hung over him. Yet the old man never wavered in his resolution[8] to part with life itself before he consented to[9] what he regarded as his daughter's dishonour.

He was sitting alone one evening pondering deeply over his troubles, and searching vainly for some way out of them. That morning had shown the figure 2 upon the wall of his house, and the next day would be the last of the allotted[10] time. What was to happen then? All manner[11] of vague and terrible fancies filled his imagination. And his daughter — what was to become of her after he was gone? Was there no escape from the invisible network[12] which was drawn all round them. He sank his head upon the table and sobbed at the thought of his own impotence[13].

What was that? In the silence he heard a gentle scratching sound — low, but very distinct in the quiet of the night. It came from the door of the house. Ferrier crept into the hall and listened intently. There was a pause for a few moments, and

1. diminuaient
2. attelage
3. courage
4. Seul
5. nul ne pouvait les emprunter
6. Où qu'il se tournât
7. il ne voyait comment éviter
8. Jamais pourtant sa résolution ne faiblit :
9. plutôt mourir que de consentir à
10. alloué
11. Toutes sortes
12. filet
13. impuissance

then the low insidious sound was repeated. Someone was evidently tapping very gently upon one of the panels of the door. Was it some midnight assassin who had come to carry out the[1] murderous orders of the secret tribunal? Or was it some agent who was marking up that the last day of grace had arrived. John Ferrier felt that instant death would be better than the suspense which shook his nerves and chilled his heart. Springing forward he drew the bolt[2] and threw the door open.

Outside all was calm and quiet. The night was fine, and the stars were twinkling brightly overhead. The little front garden lay before the farmer's eyes bounded[3] by the fence and gate, but neither there nor on the road was any human being to be seen. With a sigh of relief[4], Ferrier looked to right and to left, until happening to glance straight down at his own feet he saw to his astonishment a man lying flat upon his face upon the ground, with arms and legs all asprawl[5].

So unnerved[6] was he at the sight that he leaned up against the wall with his hand to his throat to stifle[7] his inclination[8] to call out. His first thought was that the prostrate figure[9] was that of some wounded or dying man, but as he watched it he saw it writhe along the ground[10] and into the hall[11] with the rapidity and noiselessness of a serpent. Once within the house the man sprang to his feet, closed the door, and revealed to the astonished farmer the fierce face and resolute expression of Jefferson Hope.

'Good God!' gasped[12] John Ferrier. 'How you scared me! Whatever made you come in like that?'

1. venu s'acquitter des
2. verrou
3. borné
4. soupir de soulagement
5. écartés de tout leur long
6. secoué
7. réprimer
8. envie
9. forme étendue au sol
10. se tortiller par terre
11. avancer jusqu'au vestibule
12. s'écria

'Give me food,' the other said, hoarsely[1]. 'I have had no time for bite or sup[2] for eight-and-forty hours.' He flung himself upon the cold meat and bread which were still lying upon the table from his host's supper, and devoured it voraciously. 'Does Lucy bear up well[3]?' he asked, when he had satisfied his hunger.

'Yes. She does not know the danger,' her father answered.

'That is well. The house is watched on every side. That is why I crawled my way up to it. They may be darned sharp[4], but they're not quite sharp enough to catch a Washoe hunter.'

John Ferrier felt a different man now that he realized that he had a devoted ally[5]. He seized the young man's leathery[6] hand and wrung it cordially. 'You're a man to be proud of,' he said. 'There are not many who would come to share our danger and our troubles.'

'You've hit it there, pard[7],' the young hunter answered. 'I have a respect for you, but if you were alone in this business I'd think twice before I put my head into such a hornet's nest[8]. It's Lucy that brings me here, and before harm comes on her[9] I guess there will be one less o' the Hope family in Utah.'

'What are we to do?'

'Tomorrow is your last day, and unless you act tonight you are lost. I have a mule and two horses waiting in the Eagle Ravine. How much money have you?'

'Two thousand dollars in gold, and five in notes[10].'

'That will do. I have as much more to add to it. We must push for[11] Carson City through the

1. d'une voix rauque
2. Je n'ai rien eu le temps d'avaler
3. Est-ce que Lucy tient le coup
4. sacrément malins
5. allié dévoué
6. parcheminée
7. Ça c'est sûr, partenaire
8. nid de frelons
9. avant qu'il ne lui arrive quoi que ce soit
10. billets
11. Il nous faut rallier

mountains. You had best wake Lucy. It is as well that the servants do not sleep in the house.'

While Ferrier was absent, preparing his daughter for the approaching journey[1], Jefferson Hope packed all the eatables[2] that he could find into a small parcel, and filled a stoneware[3] jar with water, for he knew by experience that the mountain wells[4] were few and far between[5]. He had hardly completed[6] his arrangements[7] before the farmer returned with his daughter all dressed and ready for a start. The greeting between the lovers was warm, but brief, for minutes were precious, and there was much to be done.

'We must make our start at once,' said Jefferson Hope, speaking in a low but resolute voice, like one who realizes the greatness of the peril, but has steeled his heart[8] to meet it[9]. 'The front and back entrances are watched, but with caution we may get away through the side window and across the fields. Once on the road we are only two miles from the Ravine where the horses are waiting. By daybreak we should be half-way through the mountains.'

'What if we are stopped[10]?' asked Ferrier.

Hope slapped[11] the revolver butt[12] which protruded[13] from the front of his tunic. 'If they are too many for us we shall take two or three of them with us,' he said with a sinister smile.

The lights inside the house had all been extinguished, and from the darkened window Ferrier peered[14] over the fields which had been his own, and which he was now about to abandon for ever. He had long nerved himself[15] to the sacrifice, however, and the thought of the honour and happiness of his daughter outweighed[16] any regret at his

1. voyage
2. vivres
3. en grès
4. sources
5. rares et éloignées les unes des autres
6. À peine avait-il achevé
7. préparatifs
8. s'est cuirassé
9. pour y faire face
10. Et si on nous arrête
11. tapota
12. crosse du revolver
13. dépassait
14. jeta un coup d'œil
15. s'était préparé de longue date
16. prévalaient largement sur

ruined fortunes. All looked so peaceful and happy, the rustling trees[1] and the broad silent stretch of grain-land[2], that it was difficult to realize that the spirit of murder lurked through it all[3]. Yet the white[4] face and set[5] expression of the young hunter showed that in his approach to the house he had seen enough to satisfy him upon that head[6].

Ferrier carried the bag of gold and notes, Jefferson Hope had the scanty[7] provisions and water, while Lucy had a small bundle containing a few of her more valued possessions. Opening the window very slowly and carefully, they waited until a dark cloud had somewhat obscured the night, and then one by one passed through into the little garden. With bated breath[8] and crouching figures[9] they stumbled across it[10], and gained the shelter of the hedge, which they skirted[11] until they came to the gap[12] which opened into the cornfields. They had just reached this point when the young man seized his two companions and dragged them down into the shadow, where they lay silent and trembling.

It was as well that his prairie training had given Jefferson Hope the ears of a lynx. He and his friends had hardly crouched down before the melancholy hooting[13] of a mountain owl was heard within a few yards of them, which was immediately answered by another hoot at a small distance. At the same moment a vague shadowy figure emerged from the gap for which they had been making[14], and uttered the plaintive signal cry again, on which[15] a second man appeared out of the obscurity.

'Tomorrow at midnight,' said the first who appeared to be in authority[16].

'When the Whip-poor-Will[17] calls three times.'

1. le bruissement des arbres
2. les vastes et silencieux champs de blé
3. y rôdait
4. blême
5. figée
6. à ce propos
7. maigres
8. Retenant leur souffle
9. courbés en deux,
10. le traversèrent comme ils purent
11. qu'ils longèrent
12. trouée
13. hululement
14. vers laquelle ils se dirigeaient
15. sur quoi
16. semblait être le chef
17. l'engoulevent

'It is well,' returned the other. 'Shall I tell Brother Drebber?'

'Pass it on to him[1], and from him to the others[2]. Nine to seven!'

'Seven to five!' repeated the other, and the two figures flitted away[3] in different directions. Their concluding words had evidently been some form of sign and countersign[4]. The instant that their footsteps had died away in the distance, Jefferson Hope sprang to his feet, and helping his companions through the gap, led the way across the fields at the top of his speed, supporting[5] and half-carrying the girl when her strength appeared to fail her[6].

'Hurry on! hurry on!' he gasped from time to time. 'We are through the line of sentinels. Everything depends on speed. Hurry on!'

Once on the high road they made rapid progress. Only once did they meet anyone, and then they managed to slip[7] into a field, and so avoid recognition. Before reaching the town the hunter branched away[8] into a rugged[9] and narrow footpath which led to the mountains. Two dark jagged peaks[10] loomed[11] above them through the darkness, and the defile which led between them was the Eagle Cañon in which the horses were awaiting them. With unerring[12] instinct Jefferson Hope picked[13] his way among the great boulders[14] and along the bed of a dried-up watercourse, until he came to the retired corner[15], screened with[16] rocks, where the faithful animals had been picketed[17]. The girl was placed upon the mule, and old Ferrier upon one of the horses, with his money-bag, while Jefferson Hope led the other along the precipitous[18] and dangerous path.

1. Passe-lui la consigne
2. et lui aux autres
3. repartirent en un instant
4. des mots de passe
5. soutenant
6. lui manquer
7. à se glisser
8. bifurqua
9. accidenté
10. pics dentelés
11. se dressaient
12. infaillible
13. repérait
14. rochers
15. l'emplacement à l'écart
16. dissimulé derrière
17. attachés
18. escarpé

It was a bewildering[1] route for anyone who was not accustomed to face Nature in her wildest moods. On the one side a great crag[2] towered up[3] a thousand feet or more, black, stern, and menacing, with long basaltic columns upon its rugged surface like the ribs[4] of some petrified monster. On the other hand a wild chaos of boulders and debris made all advance impossible. Between the two ran the irregular track, so narrow in places that they had to travel in Indian file, and so rough that only practised riders could have traversed it at all. Yet in spite of all dangers and difficulties, the hearts of the fugitives were light within them[5], for every step increased[6] the distance between them and the terrible despotism from which they were flying.

They soon had a proof, however, that they were still within the jurisdiction of the Saints[7]. They had reached the very wildest and most desolate portion of the pass when the girl gave a startled cry[8], and pointed upwards. On a rock which overlooked the track, showing out dark and plain against the sky, there stood a solitary sentinel. He saw them as soon as they perceived him, and his military challenge[9] of 'Who goes there?' rang through the silent ravine.

'Travellers for Nevada,' said Jefferson Hope, with his hand upon the rifle which hung by his saddle.

They could see the lonely watcher fingering[10] his gun, and peering down at them as if dissatisfied at their reply.

'By whose permission?' he asked.

'The Holy Four,' answered Ferrier. His Mormon experiences had taught him that that was the highest authority to which he could refer.

'Nine from seven,' cried the sentinel.

1. déstabilisante
2. pic escarpé
3. s'élevait
4. côtes
5. les fugitifs avaient le cœur léger
6. augmentait
7. dans le territoire relevant des mormons
8. cri apeuré
9. sommation
10. manipulant

'Seven from five,' returned Jefferson Hope promptly, remembering the countersign which he had heard in the garden.

'Pass, and the Lord go with you,' said the voice from above. Beyond his post the path broadened out[1], and the horses were able to break into a trot[2]. Looking back, they could see the solitary watcher leaning upon his gun, and knew that they had passed the outlying post[3] of the chosen people, and that freedom lay before them.

1. s'élargissait
2. prendre le trot
3. le poste le plus reculé

CHAPTER V

The Avenging Angels

ALL night their course lay through intricate[1] defiles and over irregular and rock-strewn[2] paths. More than once they lost their way, but Hope's intimate knowledge[3] of the mountains enabled them to regain the track[4] once more. When morning broke, a scene of marvellous though savage beauty lay before them. In every direction the great snow-capped peaks hemmed them in[5], peeping over[6] each other's shoulders to the far horizon. So steep were the rocky banks on either side of them, that the larch[7] and the pine seemed to be suspended over their heads, and to need only a gust of wind[8] to come hurtling down upon them[9]. Nor was the fear entirely an illusion, for the barren[10] valley was thickly strewn with trees and boulders which had fallen in a similar manner. Even as[11] they passed, a great rock came thundering down with a hoarse rattle[12] which woke the echoes in the silent gorges, and startled the weary horses into a gallop[13].

As the sun rose slowly above the eastern horizon, the caps of the great mountains lit up one after the other, like lamps at a festival, until they were all ruddy[14] and glowing[15]. The magnificent spectacle cheered[16] the hearts of the three fugitives and gave them fresh energy. At a wild torrent which swept out of a ravine they called a halt[17]

1. tortueux
2. couverts de pierres
3. profonde connaissance
4. piste
5. les encerclaient
6. pointant par-dessus
7. mélèze
8. bourrasque
9. pour être précipités sur eux
10. stérile
11. Au moment même où
12. dévala dans un bruit de tonnerre et un entrechoquement de rocailles
13. lança au galop les chevaux recrus de fatigue
14. rougeoyantes
15. éclatantes
16. réchauffa
17. firent halte

1. firent boire
2. tout en prenant
3. volontiers
4. doivent être sur nos talons, à l'heure qu'il est
5. le restant
6. à près de 50 km
7. s'installèrent sous un rocher en surplomb
8. blottis les uns contre les autres
9. pour se tenir chaud
10. dont ils avaient suscité l'hostilité
11. ne se doutait pas de
12. la très longue portée de cette main de fer
13. ni avec quelle rapidité
14. maigres
15. à manquer
16. peu d'inquiétude
17. du gibier
18. recoin abrité
19. 1 600 m
20. d'un froid vif
21. attaché
22. partit en quête de

and watered[1] their horses, while they partook of[2] a hasty breakfast. Lucy and her father would fain[3] have rested longer, but Jefferson Hope was inexorable. 'They will be upon our track by this time[4],' he said. 'Everything depends upon our speed. Once safe in Carson we may rest for the remainder[5] of our lives.'

During the whole of that day they struggled on through the defiles, and by evening they calculated that they were more than thirty miles[6] from their enemies. At night-time they chose the base of a beetling crag[7], where the rocks offered some protection from the chill wind, and there huddled together[8] for warmth[9], they enjoyed a few hours' sleep. Before daybreak, however, they were up and on their way once more. They had seen no signs of any pursuers, and Jefferson Hope began to think that they were fairly out of the reach of the terrible organization whose enmity they had incurred[10]. He little knew[11] how far that iron grasp could reach[12], or how soon[13] it was to close upon them and crush them.

About the middle of the second day of their flight their scanty store of[14] provisions began to run out[15]. This gave the hunter little uneasiness[16], however, for there was game to be had[17] among the mountains, and he had frequently before had to depend upon his rifle for the needs of life. Choosing a sheltered nook[18], he piled together a few dried branches and made a blazing fire, at which his companions might warm themselves, for they were now nearly five thousand feet[19] above the sea level, and the air was bitter and keen[20]. Having tethered[21] the horses, and bade Lucy adieu, he threw his gun over his shoulder, and set out in search of[22] whatever chance might throw in his way[1]. Looking back he saw the old man and the young girl crouching over the blazing fire, while the three animals stood motionless in the back-ground. Then the intervening rocks hid them from his view.

He walked for a couple of miles through one ravine after another without success, though from the marks upon the bark[2] of the trees, and other indications, he judged that there were numerous bears in the vicinity[3]. At last, after two or three hours' fruitless[4] search, he was thinking of turning back in despair, when casting his eyes upwards he saw a sight which sent a thrill[5] of pleasure through his heart. On the edge of a jutting[6] pinnacle[7], three or four hundred feet above him, there stood a creature somewhat resembling a sheep in appearance, but armed with a pair of gigantic horns. The bighorn[8] — for so it is called — was acting, probably, as a guardian over a flock[9] which were invisible to the hunter; but fortunately it was heading[10] in the opposite direction, and had not perceived him. Lying on his face[11], he rested his rifle upon a rock, and took a long and steady aim[12] before drawing the trigger[13]. The animal sprang into the air, tottered[14] for a moment upon the edge of the precipice, and then came crashing down into the valley beneath.

The creature was too unwieldy[15] to lift, so the hunter contented himself with cutting away one haunch and part of the flank. With this trophy over his shoulder, he hastened to retrace his steps[16], for the evening was already drawing in[17]. He had hardly started, however, before he realized the difficulty which faced him. In his eagerness[18] he had wandered far past the ravines which were known

1. ce que le hasard mettrait sur son chemin

2. écorce

3. aux alentours

4. infructueuse

5. frisson

6. proéminent

7. piton

8. [mouflon d'Amérique ou mouflon des Rocheuses]

9. troupeau

10. était tourné

11. Couché à plat ventre

12. visa longuement, posément

13. d'appuyer sur la détente

14. chancela

15. pesant

16. de revenir sur ses pas

17. jour baissait

18. ardeur,

to him, and it was no easy matter to pick out[1] the path which he had taken. The valley in which he found himself divided and sub-divided into many gorges, which were so like each other that it was impossible to distinguish one from the other. He followed one for a mile or more until he came to a mountain torrent which he was sure that he had never seen before. Convinced that he had taken the wrong turn, he tried another, but with the same result. Night was coming on rapidly, and it was almost dark before he at last found himself in a defile which was familiar to him. Even then it was no easy matter to keep to the right track, for the moon had not yet risen, and the high cliffs on either side[2] made the obscurity more profound. Weighed down with his burden[3], and weary from his exertions[4], he stumbled along[5], keeping up his heart by the reflection[6] that every step brought him nearer to Lucy, and that he carried with him enough to ensure them food[7] for the remainder of their journey.

He had now come to the mouth[8] of the very defile in which he had left them. Even in the darkness he could recognize the outline[9] of the cliffs which bounded it. They must, he reflected, be awaiting him anxiously, for he had been absent nearly five hours. In the gladness of his heart[10] he put his hands to his mouth and made the glen re-echo to a loud halloo[11] as a signal that he was coming. He paused and listened for an answer. None came save his own cry, which clattered up the dreary silent ravines[12], and was borne back to[13] his ears in countless repetitions. Again he shouted, even louder than before, and again no whisper came back from the friends whom he had left such a short time ago. A vague, nameless dread[14] came over

1. retrouver
2. de part et d'autre
3. Ployant sous son fardeau
4. épuisé par ses efforts
5. avançait à grand-peine
6. et s'encourageait en songeant
7. de quoi leur assurer de la nourriture
8. l'entrée
9. les contours
10. son euphorie,
11. lança un appel sonore dont l'écho résonna dans le vallon
12. qui se répercuta avec fracas dans le silence lugubre des ravins
13. revint à
14. indéfinissable appréhension

him, and he hurried onwards frantically[1], dropping the precious food in his agitation.

When he turned the corner, he came full in sight of the spot where the fire had been lit. There was still a glowing pile of wood ashes there, but it had evidently not been tended[2] since his departure. The same dead[3] silence still reigned all round. With his fears all changed to convictions, he hurried on. There was no living creature near the remains of the fire: animals, man, maiden, all were gone. It was only too clear that some sudden and terrible disaster had occurred during his absence — a disaster which had embraced them all[4], and yet had left no traces behind it.

Bewildered and stunned[5] by this blow, Jefferson Hope felt his head spin round[6], and had to lean upon his rifle to save himself from falling[7]. He was essentially a man of action, however, and speedily recovered from his temporary impotence[8]. Seizing a half-consumed piece of wood from the smouldering fire[9], he blew it into a flame, and proceeded with its help to[10] examine the little camp. The ground was all stamped down[11] by the feet of horses, showing that a large party of mounted men had overtaken[12] the fugitives, and the direction of their tracks proved that they had afterwards turned back to Salt Lake City. Had they carried back both of his companions with them? Jefferson Hope had almost persuaded himself that they must have done so, when his eye fell upon an object which made every nerve of his body tingle within him[13]. A little way on one side of the camp was a low-lying heap[14] of reddish soil, which had assuredly not been there before. There was no mistaking it for anything but a newly-dug grave[15]. As the young

1. éperdu
2. de toute évidence il n'avait pas été entretenu
3. total
4. s'était abattu sur eux tous
5. Complètement abasourdi
6. lui tourner
7. pour éviter de tomber
8. défaillance
9. feu qui se consumait
10. s'en servit pour
11. piétiné
12. rattrapé
13. le fit frissonner tout entier
14. petit amas
15. C'était, de toute évidence, une tombe creusée depuis peu

1. dans une fente à son sommet
2. sans ambages
3. qui vécut à
4. robuste
5. frénétiquement
6. accomplir
7. caractère inéluctable
8. impuissance à l'empêcher
9. en sa dernière et silencieuse demeure
10. qu'engendre le désespoir
11. Outre
12. indomptables
13. grande rancune persistante
14. seule
15. apaiser
16. douleur
17. total
18. châtiment
19. infatigable
20. seraient, décida-t-il, tournées vers ce seul but
21. ravivé

hunter approached it, he perceived that a stick had been planted on it, with a sheet of paper stuck in the cleft fork of it[1]. The inscription upon the paper was brief, but to the point[2]:

JOHN FERRIER,
Formerly of[3] Salt Lake City
Died August 4th, 1860

The sturdy[4] old man, whom he had left so short a time before, was gone, then, and this was all his epitaph. Jefferson Hope looked wildly[5] round to see if there was a second grave, but there was no sign of one. Lucy had been carried back by their terrible pursuers to fulfil[6] her original destiny, by becoming one of the harem of the Elder's son. As the young fellow realized the certainty[7] of her fate, and his own powerlessness to prevent it[8], he wished that he, too, was lying with the old farmer in his last silent resting-place[9].

Again, however, his active spirit shook off the lethargy which springs from despair[10]. If there was nothing else left to him, he could at least devote his life to revenge. With[11] indomitable[12] patience and perseverance, Jefferson Hope possessed also a power of sustained vindictiveness[13], which he may have learned from the Indians amongst whom he had lived. As he stood by the desolate fire, he felt that the only one[14] thing which could assuage[15] his grief[16] would be thorough[17] and complete retribution[18], brought by his own hand upon his enemies. His strong will and untiring[19] energy should, he determined, be devoted to that one end[20]. With a grim, white face, he retraced his steps to where he had dropped the food, and having stirred up[21] the smouldering fire, he cooked enough to last him for a few days. This he made up into a bundle, and, tired as he was[1], he set himself[2] to walk back through the mountains upon the track of the Avenging Angels.

For five days he toiled[3] footsore and weary[4] through the defiles which he had already traversed on horseback. At night he flung himself down among the rocks, and snatched[5] a few hours of sleep; but before daybreak he was always well on his way. On the sixth day, he reached the Eagle Cañon, from which they had commenced their ill-fated[6] flight. Thence he could look down upon the home of the saints. Worn and exhausted, he leaned upon his rifle and shook[7] his gaunt hand[8] fiercely[9] at the silent widespread city beneath him. As he looked at it, he observed that there were flags in some of the principal streets, and other signs of festivity. He was still speculating as to[10] what this might mean when he heard the clatter of horse's hoofs, and saw a mounted man riding towards him. As he approached, he recognized him as a Mormon named Cowper, to whom he had rendered services at different times. He therefore accosted him when he got up to him[11], with the object of finding out what Lucy Ferrier's fate had been.

'I am Jefferson Hope,' he said. 'You remember me.'

The Mormon looked at him with undisguised astonishment — indeed, it was difficult to recognize in this tattered[12], unkempt[13] wanderer, with ghastly white face and fierce, wild eyes, the spruce[14] young hunter of former days[15]. Having, however, at last, satisfied himself as to[16] his identity, the man's surprise changed to consternation.

1. malgré sa fatigue
2. se mit en demeure
3. peina,
4. las et les pieds endoloris,
5. grappillait
6. funeste
7. brandit
8. poing émacié
9. farouchement
10. en était encore à s'interroger sur
11. le cavalier arriva à sa hauteur
12. en guenilles
13. débraillé
14. fringant
15. d'antan
16. S'étant néanmoins finalement convaincu de

'You are mad to come here,' he cried. 'It is as much as my own life is worth to be seen talking with you[1]. There is a warrant[2] against you from the Holy Four for assisting the Ferriers away[3].'

'I don't fear them, or their warrant,' Hope said, earnestly. 'You must know something of this matter, Cowper. I conjure you by everything you hold dear[4] to answer a few questions. We have always been friends. For God's sake, don't refuse to answer me.'

'What is it?' the Mormon asked uneasily[5]. 'Be quick. The very rocks[6] have ears and the trees eyes.'

'What has become of Lucy Ferrier?'

'She was married yesterday to young Drebber. Hold up, man[7], hold up, you have no life left in you[8].'

'Don't mind me[9],' said Hope faintly. He was white to the very lips, and had sunk down on the stone against which he had been leaning. 'Married, you say?'

'Married yesterday — that's what those flags are for on the Endowment House[10]. There was some words between young Drebber and young Stangerson as to which was to have her. They'd both been in the party that followed them, and Stangerson had shot her father, which seemed to give him the best claim[11]; but when they argued it out in council[12], Drebber's party was the stronger, so the Prophet gave her over to him. No one won't have her very long though, for I saw death in her face yesterday. She is more like a ghost than a woman. Are you off, then[13]?'

'Yes, I am off,' said Jefferson Hope, who had risen from his seat. His face might have been chiselled

1. Te parler peut être mon arrêt de mort
2. un mandat
3. pour avoir aidé les Ferrier à s'enfuir
4. par tout ce qui t'est cher
5. mal à l'aise
6. rochers eux-mêmes
7. Tiens bon, mon gars
8. l'air au bout du rouleau
9. Ne fais pas attention à moi
10. Maison de dotation [où étaient administrées les ordonnances du temple]
11. lui donner l'avantage
12. quand le Conseil en a débattu
13. Alors, tu t'en vas

out of marble[1], so hard and set was its expression, while its eyes glowed with a baleful[2] light.

'Where are you going?'

'Never mind,' he answered; and, slinging his weapon over his shoulder, strode off down the gorge and so away into the heart of the mountains to the haunts[3] of the wild beasts. Amongst them all there was none so fierce and so dangerous as himself.

The prediction of the Mormon was only too well fulfilled[4]. Whether it was the terrible death of her father or the effects of the hateful marriage into which she had been forced, poor Lucy never held up her head again, but pined away[5] and died within a month. Her sottish husband[6], who had married her principally for the sake of[7] John Ferrier's property, did not affect any great grief at his bereavement[8]; but his other wives mourned over her[9], and sat up with her[10] the night before the burial, as is the Mormon custom. They were grouped round the bier[11] in the early hours of the morning, when, to their inexpressible[12] fear and astonishment, the door was flung open, and a savage-looking, weather-beaten[13] man in tattered garments strode into the room. Without a glance or a word to the cowering[14] women, he walked up to the white silent figure which had once contained the pure soul of Lucy Ferrier. Stooping over her, he pressed his lips reverently to her cold forehead, and then, snatching up her hand, he took the wedding-ring from her finger. 'She shall not be buried in that,' he cried with a fierce snarl[15], and before an alarm could be raised sprang down the stairs and was gone. So strange and so brief was the episode, that the watchers might have found it hard to believe it

1. taillé dans le marbre
2. funeste
3. là où sont les repaires
4. ne se réalisa que trop bien
5. dépérit
6. abruti de mari
7. parce qu'il lorgnait sur
8. lors de ce deuil
9. la pleurèrent
10. la veillèrent
11. cercueil
12. indicibles
13. tanné
14. apeurées
15. d'un ton rogue

themselves or persuade other people of it, had it not been for the undeniable fact that the circlet[1] of gold which marked her as having been a bride had disappeared.

For some months Jefferson Hope lingered[2] among the mountains, leading a strange wild life, and nursing in his heart[3] the fierce desire for vengeance which possessed him[4]. Tales were told in the City of the weird[5] figure which was seen prowling about the suburbs[6], and which haunted the lonely mountain gorges. Once a bullet whistled through Stangerson's window and flattened itself[7] upon the wall within a foot of him. On another occasion, as Drebber passed under a cliff a great boulder crashed down on him, and he only escaped a terrible death by throwing himself upon his face. The two young Mormons were not long in discovering the reason of these attempts upon their lives[8], and led repeated expeditions into the mountains in the hope of capturing or killing their enemy, but always without success. Then they adopted the precaution of never going out alone or after nightfall, and of having their houses guarded. After a time they were able to relax[9] these measures, for nothing was either heard or seen of their opponent[10], and they hoped that time had cooled his vindictiveness[11].

Far from doing so, it had, if anything,[12] augmented it. The hunter's mind was of a hard, unyielding[13] nature, and the predominant idea of revenge had taken such complete possession of it that there was no room for any other emotion. He was, however, above all things practical. He soon realized that even his iron constitution could not stand[14] the incessant strain[15] which he was

1. anneau
2. resta
3. nourrissant secrètement
4. l'habitait
5. étrange
6. rôder dans les faubourgs
7. s'écrasa
8. tentatives d'assassinat
9. assouplir
10. adversaire
11. apaisé sa soif de vengeance
12. plutôt
13. inflexible
14. supporter
15. tension

putting upon it[1]. Exposure[2] and want[3] of wholesome[4] food were wearing him out[5]. If he died like a dog among the mountains, what was to become of his revenge then? And yet such a death was sure to overtake him if he persisted. He felt that that was to play his enemy's game, so he reluctantly[6] returned to the old Nevada mines, there to recruit his health[7] and to amass money enough to allow him to pursue his object without privation.

His intention had been to be absent a year at the most, but a combination of unforeseen[8] circumstances prevented his leaving the mines for nearly five. At the end of that time, however, his memory of his wrongs[9] and his craving for[10] revenge were quite as keen[11] as on that memorable night when he had stood by John Ferrier's grave. Disguised, and under an assumed name[12], he returned to Salt Lake City, careless what became of his own life, as long as he obtained what he knew to be justice. There he found evil tidings[13] awaiting him. There had been a schism among the Chosen People a few months before, some of the younger members of the Church having rebelled against the authority of the Elders, and the result had been the secession of a certain number of the malcontents[14], who had left Utah and become Gentiles. Among these had been Drebber and Stangerson; and no one knew whither[15] they had gone. Rumour reported that Drebber had managed to convert a large part of his property into money, and that he had departed a wealthy man, while his companion, Stangerson, was comparatively poor. There was no clue at all, however, as to their whereabouts[16].

Many a man, however vindictive, would have abandoned all thought of revenge in the face of

1. qu'il lui faisait subir
2. L'exposition permanente aux intempéries
3. le manque
4. saine
5. l'épuisaient
6. à contrecœur
7. pour s'y refaire une santé
8. imprévues
9. le souvenir des injustices dont il avait été victime
10. soif de
11. vifs
12. nom d'emprunt
13. mauvaises nouvelles
14. mécontents
15. où
16. Aucun indice, cependant, ne permettait de savoir où ils se trouvaient

such a difficulty, but Jefferson Hope never faltered[1] for a moment. With the small competence[2] he possessed, eked out[3] by such employment as he could pick up[4], he travelled from town to town through the United States in quest of his enemies. Year passed into year, his black hair turned grizzled, but still he wandered on, a human bloodhound[5], with his mind wholly set[6] upon the one object upon which he had devoted his life. At last his perseverance was rewarded[7]. It was but a glance of a face in a window[8], but that one glance told him that Cleveland in Ohio possessed the men whom he was in pursuit of. He returned to his miserable lodgings with his plan of vengeance all arranged. It chanced[9], however, that Drebber, looking from his window, had recognized the vagrant[10] in the street, and had read murder in his eyes. He hurried before a justice[11] of the peace, accompanied by Stangerson, who had become his private secretary, and represented to him[12] that they were in danger of their lives from the jealousy and hatred of an old rival. That evening Jefferson Hope was taken into custody[13], and not being able to find sureties[14], was detained for some weeks. When at last he was liberated, it was only to find that Drebber's house was deserted, and that he and his secretary had departed for Europe.

Again the avenger had been foiled[15], and again his concentrated hatred urged him[16] to continue the pursuit. Funds were wanting[17], however, and for some time he had to return to work, saving[18] every dollar for his approaching journey. At last, having collected enough to keep life in him, he departed for Europe, and tracked his enemies from city to city, working his way in any menial

1. ne faiblit pas
2. pécule
3. augmenté
4. tel ou tel emploi qu'il pouvait décrocher
5. limier
6. entièrement fixé
7. récompensée
8. Ce n'était qu'un visage entraperçu à une fenêtre
9. Il se trouva
10. vagabond
11. un juge
12. lui exposa
13. appréhendé
14. faute de garant
15. C'était une nouvelle déconvenue pour le justicier
16. le poussa
17. L'argent faisait défaut
18. économisant

capacity[1], but never overtaking[2] the fugitives. When he reached St Petersburg they had departed for Paris; and when he followed them there he learned that they had just set off for Copenhagen. At the Danish capital he was again a few days late, for they had journeyed on to London, where he at last succeeded in running them to earth[3]. As to what occurred there, we cannot do better than quote[4] the old hunter's own account[5], as duly recorded[6] in Dr Watson's Journal, to which we are already under such obligations[7].

1. prenant n'importe quel humble emploi pour lui permettre d'avancer
2. sans jamais rattraper
3. à les débusquer
4. citer
5. récit
6. tel qu'il est dûment consigné
7. auquel nous devons déjà tant

CHAPTER VI

A Continuation of the Reminiscences of John Watson, M.D.

OUR prisoner's furious resistance did not apparently indicate any ferocity in his disposition towards ourselves, for on finding himself powerless, he smiled in an affable manner, and expressed his hopes that he had not hurt any of us in the scuffle[1]. 'I guess you're going to take me to the police-station,' he remarked to Sherlock Holmes. 'My cab's at the door. If you'll loose[2] my legs I'll walk down to it. I'm not so light to lift as I used to be.'

Gregson and Lestrade exchanged glances as if they thought this proposition rather a bold one[3]; but Holmes at once took the prisoner at his word, and loosened the towel which we had bound round his ankles. He rose and stretched his legs, as though to assure himself that they were free once more. I remember that I thought to myself, as I eyed him, that I had seldom seen a more powerfully built man; and his dark sunburned face bore an expression of determination and energy which was as formidable[4] as his personal strength.

'If there's a vacant place for a chief of the police, I reckon you are the man for it[5],' he said, gazing with undisguised admiration at my fellow-lodger[6]. 'The way you kept on my trail[7] was a caution[8].'

1. bagarre
2. voulez bien me libérer
3. audacieuse
4. impressionnante
5. je dirais que vous êtes le mieux placé
6. colocataire
7. La façon dont vous êtes resté à mes trousses
8. est remarquable

'You had better come with me,' said Holmes to the two detectives.

'I can drive you,' said Lestrade.

'Good! and Gregson can come inside with me. You too, Doctor, you have taken an interest in the case and may as well stick to us[1].'

I assented[2] gladly, and we all descended together. Our prisoner made no attempt at escape, but stepped calmly into the cab which had been his, and we followed him. Lestrade mounted the box[3], whipped up[4] the horse, and brought us in a very short time to our destination. We were ushered[5] into a small chamber where a police Inspector noted down our prisoner's name and the names of the men with whose murder he had been charged[6]. The official was a white-faced unemotional man, who went through his duties in a dull mechanical way. 'The prisoner will be put[7] before the magistrates in the course of the week,' he said; 'in the meantime[8], Mr. Jefferson Hope, have you anything that you wish to say? I must warn you that your words will be taken down[9], and may be used[10] against you.'

'I've got a good deal to say,' our prisoner said slowly. 'I want to tell you gentlemen all about it.'

'Hadn't you better reserve that for your trial[11]?' asked the Inspector.

'I may never be tried[12],' he answered. 'You needn't look startled[13]. It isn't suicide I am thinking of. Are you a Doctor?' He turned his fierce dark eyes upon me as he asked this last question.

'Yes; I am,' I answered.

'Then put your hand here,' he said, with a smile, motioning with his manacled[14] wrists towards his chest.

1. rester avec nous
2. acquiesçai
3. s'installa à la place du cocher
4. fouetta
5. On nous fit entrer
6. qu'il était accusé d'avoir assassinés
7. comparaîtra
8. en attendant
9. enregistrées
10. pourront être retenues
11. procès
12. Peut-être n'y aura-t-il pas de procès
13. étonné
14. menottés

I did so; and became at once conscious of an extraordinary throbbing[1] and commotion[2] which was going on inside. The walls of his chest seemed to thrill[3] and quiver[4] as a frail building would do inside when some powerful engine was at work. In the silence of the room I could hear a dull humming and buzzing noise[5] which proceeded[6] from the same source.

'Why,' I cried, 'you have an aortic aneurism[7]!'

'That's what they call it,' he said, placidly. 'I went to a doctor last week about it, and he told me that it is bound to burst[8] before many days passed[9]. It has been getting worse for years. I got it from over-exposure[10] and under-feeding[11] among the Salt Lake Mountains. I've done my work now, and I don't care how soon I go, but I should like to leave some account of the business[12] behind me. I don't want to be remembered as a common cut-throat[13].'

The inspector and the two detectives had a hurried discussion as to the advisability[14] of allowing him to tell his story.

'Do you consider, Doctor, that there is immediate danger?' the former asked.

'Most certainly there is,' I answered.

'In that case it is clearly our duty, in the interests of justice, to take his statement[15],' said the inspector. 'You are at liberty[16], sir, to give your account, which I again warn you will be taken down.'

'I'll sit down, with your leave[17],' the prisoner said, suiting the action to the word[18]. 'This aneurism of mine makes me easily tired, and the tussle[19] we had half an hour ago has not mended[20] matters. I'm on the brink of the grave[21], and I am not likely to lie to you. Every word I say is the absolute

1. palpitations
2. agitation
3. frémir
4. trembler
5. bourdonnement sourd
6. provenait
7. anévrisme de l'aorte
8. éclaterait inévitablement
9. sous peu
10. surexposition aux intempéries
11. sous-alimentation
12. quelques explications sur toute cette affaire
13. vulgaire assassin
14. opportunité
15. déposition
16. autorisé
17. permission
18. et il joignit l'acte à la parole
19. l'empoignade
20. arrangé
21. J'ai un pied dans la tombe

truth, and how you use it is a matter of no consequence to me[1].'

With these words, Jefferson Hope leaned back in his chair and began the following remarkable statement. He spoke in a calm and methodical manner, as though the events which he narrated were commonplace enough[2]. I can vouch for[3] the accuracy[4] of the subjoined[5] account, for I have had access to Lestrade's notebook, in which the prisoner's words were taken down exactly as they were uttered.

'It don't much matter to you why I hated these men,' he said; 'it's enough that they were guilty[6] of the death of two human beings — a father and a daughter — and that they had, therefore, forfeited[7] their own lives. After the lapse of time that has passed since their crime, it was impossible for me to secure a conviction against them[8] in any court. I knew of their guilt though, and I determined that I should be judge, jury, and executioner[9] all rolled into one[10]. You'd have done the same, if you have any manhood[11] in you, if you had been in my place.

'That girl that I spoke of was to have married me twenty years ago. She was forced into marrying that same Drebber, and broke her heart over it[12]. I took the marriage ring from her dead finger, and I vowed[13] that his dying eyes should rest upon that very ring, and that his last thoughts should be of the crime for which he was punished. I have carried it about with me, and have followed him and his accomplice[14] over two continents until I caught them. They thought to tire me out[15], but they could not do it. If I die to-morrow, as is likely enough, I die knowing that my work in this world is done, and well done. They have perished, and

1. m'est indifférent
2. très ordinaires
3. attester de
4. exactitude
5. ci-joint
6. coupables
7. perdu tout droit à
8. d'obtenir qu'ils soient condamnés
9. bourreau
10. à moi seul
11. courage
12. en a eu le cœur brisé
13. j'ai juré
14. complice
15. que je me fatiguerais

by my hand. There is nothing left for me to hope for, or to desire.

'They were rich and I was poor, so that it was no easy matter for me to follow them. When I got to London my pocket was about[1] empty, and I found that I must turn my hand to something for my living[2]. Driving and riding are as natural to me as walking, so I applied at a[3] cabowner's office[4], and soon got employment. I was to bring a certain sum a week to the owner, and whatever was over that I might keep for myself[5]. There was seldom much over, but I managed to scrape along somehow[6]. The hardest job was to learn my way about[7], for I reckon that of all the mazes[8] that ever were contrived[9], this city is the most confusing. I had a map beside me though, and when once I had spotted[10] the principal hotels and stations, I got on pretty well.

'It was some time before I found out where my two gentlemen were living; but I inquired and inquired until at last I dropped across them[11]. They were at a boarding-house[12] at Camberwell, over on the other side of the river. When once I found them out I knew that I had them at my mercy. I had grown my beard, and there was no chance of their recognizing me. I would dog them[13] and follow them until I saw my opportunity[14]. I was determined that they should not escape me again.

'They were very near doing it for all that[15]. Go where they would about[16] London, I was always at their heels. Sometimes I followed them on my cab, and sometimes on foot, but the former was the best, for then they could not get away from me. It was only early in the morning or late at night that I could earn anything, so that I began to get

1. pour ainsi dire
2. faire quelque chose pour gagner ma vie
3. je me suis présenté au
4. bureau d'un propriétaire de fiacres
5. je pouvais garder le surplus
6. à joindre les deux bouts
7. à trouver mon chemin dans la ville
8. labyrinthes
9. conçus
10. j'eus repéré
11. tomber sur eux
12. pension
13. J'allais les filer
14. jusqu'à ce que l'occasion se présente
15. malgré tout
16. Où qu'ils aillent dans

behindhand with[1] my employer. I did not mind that, however, as long as I could lay my hand upon the men I wanted.

'They were very cunning[2], though. They must have thought that there was some chance[3] of their being followed, for they would never go out alone, and never after nightfall. During two weeks I drove behind them every day, and never once saw them separate. Drebber himself was drunk half the time, but Stangerson was not to be caught napping[4]. I watched them late and early[5], but never saw the ghost of a chance[6]; but I was not discouraged, for something told me that the hour had almost come. My only fear was that this thing in my chest might burst a little too soon and leave my work undone.

'At last, one evening I was driving up and down Torquay Terrace, as the street was called in which they boarded[7], when I saw a cab drive up to their door. Presently some luggage was brought out, and after a time Drebber and Stangerson followed it, and drove off. I whipped up my horse and kept within sight of them, feeling very ill at ease, for I feared that they were going to shift their quarters[8]. At Euston Station they got out, and I left a boy to hold my horse, and followed them on to the platform[9]. I heard them ask for the Liverpool train, and the guard answer that one had just gone and there would not be another for[10] some hours. Stangerson seemed to be put out at that[11], but Drebber was rather pleased than otherwise[12]. I got so close to them in the bustle[13] that I could hear every word that passed between them. Drebber said that he had a little business of his own to do, and that if the other would wait for him he would soon rejoin him. His companion remonstrated with him[14],

1. à devoir de l'argent à
2. rusés
3. risque
4. était toujours sur le qui-vive
5. ne relâchai jamais ma surveillance
6. l'ombre d'une occasion
7. étaient logés
8. ne changent de logement
9. quai
10. avant
11. en parut contrarié
12. qu'autre chose
13. cohue
14. protesta

and reminded him that they had resolved to stick together. Drebber answered that the matter was a delicate one, and that he must go alone. I could not catch what Stangerson said to that, but the other burst out swearing, and reminded him that he was nothing more than his paid servant, and that he must not presume to dictate to him[1]. On that the Secretary gave it up as a bad job[2], and simply bargained with him[3] that if he missed the last train he should rejoin him at Halliday's Private Hotel; to which Drebber answered that he would be back on the platform before eleven, and made his way out of the station.

'The moment for which I had waited so long had at last come. I had my enemies within my power. Together they could protect each other, but singly[4] they were at my mercy. I did not act, however, with undue precipitation. My plans were already formed. There is no satisfaction in vengeance unless the offender[5] has time to realize who it is that strikes him, and why retribution has come upon him[6]. I had my plans arranged by which I should have the opportunity of making the man who had wronged me understand that his old sin had found him out[7]. It chanced[8] that some days before a gentleman who had been engaged in looking over some houses in the Brixton Road had dropped the key of one of them in my carriage. It was claimed[9] that same evening, and returned[10]; but in the interval I had taken a moulding[11] of it, and had a duplicate constructed[12]. By means of this[13] I had access to at least one spot in this great city where I could rely upon being free from interruption. How to get Drebber to that house was the difficult problem which I had now to solve.

1. qu'il n'avait pas à lui donner des ordres
2. laissa tomber l'affaire
3. convint simplement avec lui
4. séparément
5. coupable
6. le châtiment s'abat sur lui
7. ancien forfait l'avait rattrapé
8. Il se trouvait
9. réclamée
10. restituée
11. empreinte
12. en avais fait faire un double
13. De la sorte,

'He walked down the road and went into one or two liquor shops, staying for nearly half-an-hour in the last of them. When he came out he staggered[1] in his walk, and was evidently pretty well on[2]. There was a hansom[3] just in front of me, and he hailed it. I followed it so close[4] that the nose of my horse was within a yard of his driver the whole way. We rattled across Waterloo Bridge and through miles of streets, until, to my astonishment, we found ourselves back in the Terrace in which he had boarded. I could not imagine what his intention was in returning there; but I went on and pulled up[5] my cab a hundred yards or so from the house. He entered it, and his hansom drove away. Give me a glass of water, if you please. My mouth gets dry with the talking.'

I handed him the glass, and he drank it down.

'That's better,' he said. 'Well, I waited for a quarter of an hour, or more, when suddenly there came a noise like people struggling inside the house. Next moment the door was flung open and two men appeared, one of whom was Drebber, and the other was a young chap whom I had never seen before. This fellow had Drebber by the collar[6], and when they came to the head of the steps he gave him a shove[7] and a kick which sent him half across the road. 'You hound[8],' he cried, shaking his stick at him[9]; 'I'll teach you to insult an honest girl!' He was so hot[10] that I think he would have thrashed[11] Drebber with his cudgel[12], only that the cur[13] staggered away down the road as fast as his legs would carry him. He ran as far as the corner, and then, seeing my cab, he hailed me and jumped in. 'Drive me to Halliday's Private Hotel,' said he.

1. titubait
2. visiblement bien éméché
3. fiacre
4. de si près
5. arrêtai
6. tenait Drebber par le collet
7. bourrade
8. Ordure
9. en le menaçant de sa canne
10. remonté
11. roué de coups
12. gourdin
13. mais le malotru

1. le vis bien installé
2. au point que je craignis qu'
3. besoin d'alcool
4. en m'enjoignant de l'attendre
5. tellement soûl
6. que j'avais tous les atouts en main
7. que justice
8. m'y résoudre
9. décidé depuis longtemps
10. une chance de s'en sortir
11. emplois
12. gardien
13. balayeur au
14. donnait un cours
15. dose la plus infime
16. repérai
17. j'en prélevai une petite quantité
18. préparateur
19. fabriquai, avec cet alcaloïde,
20. l'occasion se présenterait
21. chacun de ces messieurs pourrait choisir une pilule dans

'When I had him fairly inside[1] my cab, my heart jumped so with joy that I feared lest[2] at this last moment my aneurism might go wrong. I drove along slowly, weighing in my own mind what it was best to do. I might take him right out into the country, and there in some deserted lane have my last interview with him. I had almost decided upon this, when he solved the problem for me. The craze for drink[3] had seized him again, and he ordered me to pull up outside a gin palace. He went in, leaving word that I should wait for him[4]. There he remained until closing time, and when he came out he was so far gone[5] that I knew the game was in my own hands[6].

'Don't imagine that I intended to kill him in cold blood. It would only have been rigid justice[7] if I had done so, but I could not bring myself to do it[8]. I had long determined[9] that he should have a show for his life[10] if he chose to take advantage of it. Among the many billets[11] which I have filled in America during my wandering life, I was once janitor[12] and sweeper out of the[13] laboratory at York College. One day the professor was lecturing[14] on poisons, and he showed his students some alkaloid, as he called it, which he had extracted from some South American arrow poison, and which was so powerful that the least grain[15] meant instant death. I spotted[16] the bottle in which this preparation was kept, and when they were all gone, I helped myself to a little of it[17]. I was a fairly good dispenser[18], so I worked this alkaloid into[19] small, soluble pills, and each pill I put in a box with a similar pill made without the poison. I determined at the time that when I had my chance[20], my gentlemen should each have a draw out of[21] one of these boxes, while I ate the pill that remained. It would be quite as deadly[1], and a good deal less noisy than firing across a handkerchief. From that day I had always my pill boxes about with me, and the time had now come when I was to use them.

'It was nearer one than twelve, and a wild, bleak[2] night, blowing hard and raining in torrents. Dismal as it was outside[3], I was glad within — so glad that I could have shouted out from pure exultation. If any of you gentlemen have ever pined for a thing[4], and longed for it during twenty long years, and then suddenly found it within your reach, you would understand my feelings. I lit a cigar, and puffed at it[5] to steady my[6] nerves, but my hands were trembling, and my temples[7] throbbing[8] with excitement. As I drove, I could see old John Ferrier and sweet Lucy looking at me out of the darkness and smiling at me, just as plain[9] as I see you all in this room. All the way they were ahead of me, one on each side of the horse until I pulled up at the house in the Brixton Road.

'There was not a soul to be seen[10], nor a sound to be heard, except the dripping of the rain. When I looked in at the window, I found Drebber all huddled together[11] in a drunken sleep[12]. I shook him by the arm, "It's time to get out," I said.

' "All right, cabby[13]," said he.

'I suppose he thought we had come to the hotel that he had mentioned, for he got out without another word, and followed me down the garden. I had to walk beside him to keep him steady, for he was still a little top-heavy[14]. When we came to the door, I opened it, and led him into the front room. I give you my word that all the way, the father and the daughter were walking in front of us.

1. létal
2. désolée
3. Aussi lugubre que fût le temps au-dehors
4. avez jamais ardemment souhaité quelque chose
5. tirai dessus
6. pour me calmer les
7. tempes
8. battaient
9. distinctement
10. Il n'y avait personne en vue
11. tassé sur lui-même
12. sommeil d'ivrogne
13. cocher
14. chancelant

‘ “It’s infernally dark,” said he, stamping about[1].

‘ “We’ll soon have a light,” I said, striking a match and putting it to a wax candle which I had brought with me. “Now, Enoch Drebber,” I continued, turning to him, and holding the light to my own face, ‘who am I?”

‘He gazed at me with bleared[2], drunken eyes for a moment, and then I saw a horror[3] spring up in them, and convulse his whole features[4], which showed me that he knew me. He staggered back with a livid face, and I saw the perspiration break out upon his brow, while his teeth chattered[5] in his head. At the sight, I leaned my back against the door and laughed loud and long. I had always known that vengeance would be sweet, but I had never hoped for the contentment of soul[6] which now possessed me.

‘ “You dog!” I said; “I have hunted you from Salt Lake City to St Petersburg, and you have always escaped me. Now, at last your wanderings have come to an end, for either you or I shall never see tomorrow’s sun rise.” He shrunk still further away as I spoke, and I could see on his face that he thought I was mad. So I was for the time[7]. The pulses in my temples beat like sledge-hammers[8], and I believe I would have had a fit of some sort[9] if the blood had not gushed[10] from my nose and relieved me[11].

‘ “What do you think of Lucy Ferrier now?” I cried, locking the door, and shaking the key in his face. “Punishment has been slow in coming, but it has overtaken you at last[12].” I saw his coward[13] lips tremble as I spoke. He would have begged for his life[14], but he knew well that it was useless.

‘ “Would you murder me?” he stammered.

1. en marchant dans la pièce à pas lourds
2. troubles
3. l’épouvante
4. déformer ses traits
5. il claquait des dents
6. satisfaction de l’âme
7. à cet instant
8. violemment
9. fait un malaise
10. n’avait jailli
11. ne m’avait soulagé
12. t’a enfin rattrapé
13. de poltron
14. m’aurait bien supplié de lui laisser la vie sauve

' "There is no murder," I answered. "Who talks of murdering a mad dog? What mercy had you upon my poor darling, when you dragged her from her slaughtered father[1], and bore her away to your accursed[2] and shameless[3] harem."

' "It was not I who killed her father," he cried.

' "But it was you who broke her innocent heart," I shrieked[4], thrusting the box before him. "Let the high God judge between us. Choose and eat. There is death in one and life in the other. I shall take what you leave. Let us see if there is justice upon the earth, or if we are ruled by chance[5]."

'He cowered away[6] with wild cries and prayers for mercy, but I drew my knife and held it to his throat until he had obeyed me. Then I swallowed the other, and we stood facing one another in silence for a minute or more, waiting to see which was to live and which was to die. Shall I ever forget the look which came over his face when the first warning pangs[7] told him that the poison was in his system[8]? I laughed as I saw it, and held Lucy's marriage ring in front of his eyes. It was but for a moment[9], for the action of the alkaloid is rapid. A spasm of pain contorted[10] his features; he threw his hands out in front of him, staggered, and then, with a hoarse cry, fell heavily upon the floor. I turned him over with my foot, and placed my hand upon his heart. There was no movement. He was dead!

'The blood had been streaming from my nose, but I had taken no notice of it. I don't know what it was that put it into my head[11] to write upon the wall with it. Perhaps it was some mischievous[12] idea of setting the police upon a wrong track, for I felt light-hearted and cheerful. I remembered a German being found in New York with RACHE

1. tu l'as arrachée à son père assassiné
2. maudit
3. infâme
4. criai-je
5. seul règne le hasard
6. se déroba
7. douleurs annonciatrices
8. organisme
9. très bref
10. tordit
11. ce qui me prit
12. malicieuse

written up above him, and it was argued at the time[1] in the newspapers that the secret societies must have done it. I guessed that what puzzled[2] the New Yorkers would puzzle the Londoners, so I dipped my finger in my own blood and printed it on a convenient place on the wall. Then I walked down to my cab and found that there was nobody about, and that the night was still very wild. I had driven some distance when I put my hand into the pocket in which I usually kept Lucy's ring, and found that it was not there. I was thunderstruck at this[3], for it was the only memento[4] that I had of her. Thinking that I might have dropped it when I stooped over Drebber's body, I drove back, and leaving my cab in a side[5] street, I went boldly up to the house — for I was ready to dare[6] anything rather than lose the ring. When I arrived there, I walked right into the arms of a police-officer who was coming out, and only managed to disarm his suspicions[7] by pretending to be hopelessly[8] drunk.

'That was how Enoch Drebber came to his end. All I had to do then was to do as much for Stangerson, and so pay off John Ferrier's debt[9]. I knew that he was staying at Halliday's Private Hotel, and I hung about[10] all day, but he never came out. I fancy that he suspected something when Drebber failed to put in an appearance[11]. He was cunning, was Stangerson[12], and always on his guard. If he thought he could keep me off[13] by staying indoors he was very much mistaken. I soon found out which was the window of his bedroom, and early next morning I took advantage of some ladders which were lying in the lane behind the hotel, and so made my way[14] into his room in the grey of the dawn. I woke him up and told him that

1. qu'on avait affirmé à l'époque
2. avait dérouté
3. J'en fus atterré
4. souvenir
5. adjacente
6. braver
7. endormir ses soupçons
8. complètement
9. m'acquitter de la dette envers John Ferrier
10. restai aux abords
11. il vit que Drebber ne revenait pas
12. malin, ce Stangerson
13. m'échapper
14. pénétrai

the hour had come when he was to answer for[1] the life he had taken so long before. I described Drebber's death to him, and I gave him the same choice of the poisoned pills. Instead of grasping at the chance of safety[2] which that offered him, he sprang from his bed and flew at my throat. In self-defence I stabbed him to the heart. It would have been the same in any case, for Providence would never have allowed his guilty hand to pick out anything but[3] the poison.

'I have little more to say, and it's as well, for I am about done up[4]. I went on cabbing it[5] for a day or so, intending to keep at it[6] until I could save enough to take me back to America. I was standing in the yard when a ragged youngster asked if there was a cabby there called Jefferson Hope, and said that his cab was wanted[7] by a gentleman at 221B, Baker Street. I went round, suspecting no harm, and the next thing I knew[8], this young man here had the bracelets on my wrists[9], and as neatly shackled as ever I saw in my life[10]. That's the whole of my story, gentlemen. You may consider me to be a murderer; but I hold that I am[11] just as much an officer of justice as you are[12].'

So thrilling[13] had the man's narrative been, and his manner was so impressive that we had sat silent and absorbed. Even the professional detectives, *blasé* as they were[14] in every detail of crime, appeared to be keenly interested in the man's story. When he finished we sat for some minutes in a stillness which was only broken by the scratching[15] of Lestrade's pencil as he gave the finishing touches to his shorthand account[16].

'There is only one point on which I should like a little more information,' Sherlock Holmes said at

1. rendre compte de

2. saisir sa chance de salut

3. de choisir autre chose que

4. exténué

5. mon travail de cocher

6. continuer ainsi

7. demandé

8. l'instant d'après

9. m'avait passé les menottes

10. avec une adresse incroyable

11. prétends être,

12. tout autant que vous, un officier de justice

13. captivant

14. aussi blasés fussent-ils

15. grattement

16. compte rendu en sténo

last. 'Who was your accomplice who came for the ring which I advertised[1]?'

The prisoner winked at my friend jocosely[2]. 'I can tell my own secrets,' he said, 'but I don't get other people into trouble[3]. I saw your advertisement, and I thought it might be a plant[4], or it might be the ring which I wanted. My friend volunteered to go and see. I think you'll own[5] he did it smartly[6].'

'Not a doubt of that,' said Holmes heartily[7].

'Now, gentlemen,' the inspector remarked gravely, 'the forms of the law must be complied with[8]. On Thursday the prisoner will be brought[9] before the magistrates, and your attendance[10] will be required. Until then I will be responsible for him.' He rang the bell as he spoke, and Jefferson Hope was led off by a couple of warders[11], while my friend and I made our way out of the Station and took a cab back to Baker Street.

1. pour lequel j'avais passé une annonce
2. fit à mon ami un clin d'œil rieur
3. ne veux pas attirer des ennuis aux autres
4. traquenard
5. que vous reconnaîtrez
6. très adroitement
7. de bon cœur
8. respectées
9. comparaîtra
10. présence
11. gardiens

CHAPTER VII

The Conclusion

WE had all been warned to appear[1] before the magistrates upon the Thursday; but when the Thursday came there was no occasion for our testimony[2]. A higher Judge had taken the matter in hand, and Jefferson Hope had been summoned[3] before a tribunal where strict[4] justice would be meted out to him[5]. On the very night after his capture the aneurism burst, and he was found in the morning stretched upon the floor of the cell, with a placid smile upon his face, as though he had been able in his dying moments to look back upon a useful life, and on work well done.

'Gregson and Lestrade will be wild about his death[6],' Holmes remarked, as we chatted it over[7] next evening. 'Where will their grand advertisement[8] be now?'

'I don't see that they had very much to do with his capture,' I answered.

'What you do in this world is a matter of no consequence[9],' returned my companion, bitterly. 'The question is, what can you make people believe that you have done. Never mind,' he continued, more brightly, after a pause. 'I would not have missed the investigation for anything. There has been no better case within my recollection[10]. Simple as it

1. convoqués

2. notre témoignage n'était plus nécessaire

3. assigné à comparaître

4. rigoureuse

5. lui serait appliquée

6. furieux de le savoir mort

7. bavardions de l'affaire

8. réclame

9. sans importance

10. Je n'ai pas souvenir d'une affaire aussi intéressante

was, there were several most instructive points about it.'

'Simple!' I ejaculated[1].

'Well, really, it can hardly be described as otherwise,' said Sherlock Holmes, smiling at my surprise. 'The proof of its intrinsic simplicity is, that without any help save a few very ordinary deductions I was able to lay my hand upon the criminal within three days.'

'That is true,' said I.

'I have already explained to you that what is out of the common is usually a guide rather than a hindrance[2]. In solving[3] a problem of this sort, the grand thing[4] is to be able to reason backwards[5]. That is a very useful accomplishment[6], and a very easy one, but people do not practise it much. In the every-day affairs of life it is more useful to reason forwards[7], and so the other comes to be neglected. There are fifty who can reason synthetically for one who can reason analytically.'

'I confess,' said I, 'that I do not quite follow you.'

'I hardly expected that you would. Let me see if I can make it clearer. Most people, if you describe a train of events[8] to them, will tell you what the result would be. They can put those events together in their minds, and argue from them that something will come to pass[9]. There are few people, however, who, if you told them a result, would be able to evolve from their own inner consciousness what the steps were[10] which led up to that result. This power is what I mean when I talk of reasoning backwards, or analytically.'

'I understand,' said I.

'Now this was a case in which you were given the result and had to find everything else for your-

1. m'exclamai-je
2. obstacle
3. Pour résoudre
4. l'essentiel
5. raisonner à rebours
6. savoir-faire
7. de l'avant
8. succession d'événements
9. et en inférer une conséquence
10. induire de ce qu'ils savent les étapes

self. Now let me endeavour[1] to show you the different steps in my reasoning. To begin at the beginning. I approached the house, as you know, on foot, and with my mind entirely free from all impressions. I naturally began by examining the roadway, and there, as I have already explained to you, I saw clearly the marks of a cab, which, I ascertained by inquiry[2], must have been there during the night. I satisfied myself that it was a cab and not a private carriage by the narrow gauge[3] of the wheels. The ordinary London growler[4] is considerably less wide than a gentleman's brougham[5].

'This was the first point gained[6]. I then walked slowly down the garden path, which happened to be composed of a clay soil, peculiarly suitable for taking impressions[7]. No doubt it appeared to you to be a mere trampled line of slush[8], but to my trained eyes every mark upon its surface had a meaning. There is no branch of detective science which is so important and so much neglected as the art of tracing footsteps[9]. Happily, I have always laid great stress upon it[10], and much practice has made it second nature to me. I saw the heavy footmarks of the constables, but I saw also the track of the two men who had first passed through the garden. It was easy to tell that they had been before the others, because in places their marks had been entirely obliterated[11] by the others coming upon the top of them. In this way my second link was formed[12], which told me that[13] the nocturnal visitors were two in number, one remarkable for his height (as I calculated from the length of his stride), and the other fashionably dressed[14], to judge from the small and elegant impression left by his boots.

1. Je vais maintenant m'efforcer
2. m'en suis assuré par des questions
3. faible écartement
4. cabriolet
5. voiture de maître
6. acquis
7. qui restitue particulièrement bien les empreintes
8. simple allée boueuse abondamment piétinée
9. d'identifier les empreintes de pas
10. y ai toujours attaché beaucoup d'importance
11. effacées
12. C'est ainsi que j'ai pu établir mon deuxième élément
13. selon lequel
14. vêtu avec élégance

1. déduction
2. chaussé de belles bottes
3. aucune blessure
4. inquiète
5. vu le sort qui lui était réservé
6. aigrelette
7. qu'on l'avait forcé à s'empoisonner
8. Par élimination
9. ne s'accordait aux faits
10. du jamais-vu
11. par la force
12. viendront immédiatement à l'esprit
13. du mobile
14. J'ai penché, dès le début, pour
15. en prenant tout son temps
16. son auteur
17. un tort d'ordre privé
18. avait motivé

'On entering the house this last inference[1] was confirmed. My well-booted[2] man lay before me. The tall one, then, had done the murder, if murder there was. There was no wound[3] upon the dead man's person, but the agitated[4] expression upon his face assured me that he had foreseen his fate before it came upon him[5]. Men who die from heart disease, or any sudden natural cause, never by any chance exhibit agitation upon their features. Having sniffed the dead man's lips I detected a slightly sour[6] smell, and I came to the conclusion that he had had poison forced upon him[7]. Again, I argued that it had been forced upon him from the hatred and fear expressed upon his face. By the method of exclusion[8], I had arrived at this result, for no other hypothesis would meet the facts[9]. Do not imagine that it was a very unheard-of idea[10]. The forcible[11] administration of poison is by no means a new thing in criminal annals. The cases of Dolsky in Odessa, and of Leturier in Montpellier, will occur at once[12] to any toxicologist.

'And now came the great question as to the reason why[13]. Robbery had not been the object of the murder, for nothing was taken. Was it politics, then, or was it a woman? That was the question which confronted me. I was inclined from the first to[14] the latter supposition. Political assassins are only too glad to do their work and to fly. This murder had, on the contrary, been done most deliberately[15], and the perpetrator[16] had left his tracks all over the room, showing that he had been there all the time. It must have been a private wrong[17], and not a political one, which called for[18] such a methodical revenge. When the inscription was discovered upon the wall I was more inclined than ever to my opinion. The thing was too evidently a blind[1]. When the ring was found, however, it settled[2] the question. Clearly the murderer had used it to remind his victim of some dead or absent woman. It was at this point that I asked Gregson whether he had enquired[3] in his telegram to Cleveland as to any particular point in[4] Mr. Drebber's former career[5]. He answered, you remember, in the negative.

'I then proceeded to make a careful examination of the room, which confirmed me in my opinion as to the murderer's height, and furnished me with[6] the additional details as to the Trichinopoly cigar and the length of his nails. I had already come to the conclusion, since there were no signs of a struggle, that the blood which covered the floor had burst from the murderer's nose in his excitement. I could perceive that the track of blood coincided with the track of his feet. It is seldom that any man, unless he is very full-blooded[7], breaks out in this way through emotion[8], so I hazarded the opinion[9] that the criminal was probably a robust and ruddy-faced[10] man. Events proved that I had judged correctly.

'Having left the house, I proceeded to do what Gregson had neglected. I telegraphed to the head[11] of the police at Cleveland, limiting my enquiry[12] to the circumstances connected with the marriage of Enoch Drebber. The answer was conclusive[13]. It told me that Drebber had already applied for[14] the protection of the law against an old rival in love, named Jefferson Hope, and that this same Hope was at present in Europe. I knew now that I held the clue to the mystery in my hand, and all that remained was to secure the[15] murderer.

1. leurre
2. cela a réglé
3. s'il avait demandé
4. des détails sur
5. le passé
6. m'a fourni
7. sanguin
8. manifeste son émotion de telle sorte
9. j'ai risqué l'hypothèse
10. rougeaud
11. au chef
12. requête
13. probante
14. demandé à bénéficier de
15. s'emparer du

'I had already determined[1] in my own mind that the man who had walked into the house with Drebber was none other than the man who had driven the cab. The marks in the road showed me that the horse had wandered on[2] in a way which would have been impossible had there been anyone in charge of it[3]. Where, then, could the driver be, unless he were inside the house? Again, it is absurd to suppose that any sane[4] man would carry out a deliberate crime under the very eyes, as it were[5], of a third person, who was sure to betray him[6]. Lastly, supposing one man wished to dog another[7] through London, what better means could he adopt than to turn[8] cabdriver. All these considerations led me to the irresistible[9] conclusion that Jefferson Hope was to be found among the jarveys[10] of the Metropolis[11].

'If he had been one, there was no reason to believe that he had ceased to be. On the contrary, from his point of view, any sudden change would be likely to draw attention to himself. He would, probably, for a time at least, continue to perform his duties[12]. There was no reason to suppose that he was going under an assumed name[13]. Why should he change his name in a country where no one knew his original one? I therefore organized my Street Arab detective corps[14], and sent them systematically to every cab proprietor in London until they ferreted out[15] the man that I wanted. How well they succeeded[16], and how quickly I took advantage of it[17], are still fresh in your recollection. The murder of Stangerson was an incident which was entirely unexpected, but which could hardly in any case have been prevented[18]. Through it[19], as you know, I came into possession of the pills, the

1. établi
2. avait marché de-ci de-là
3. s'il y avait eu quelqu'un pour le diriger
4. sain d'esprit
5. pour ainsi dire sous les yeux
6. n'aurait pas manqué de le trahir
7. en prendre un autre en filature
8. que de se faire
9. indiscutable
10. cochers
11. capitale
12. à faire son travail
13. nom d'emprunt
14. équipe de petits détectives des rues
15. débusquent
16. Leur pleine réussite
17. la rapidité avec laquelle j'en ai tiré parti
18. empêché
19. Grâce à ce meurtre

existence of which I had already surmised[1]. You see the whole thing is a chain of logical sequences without a break or flaw[2].'

'It is wonderful!' I cried. 'Your merits should be publicly recognized. You should publish an account of the case. If you won't, I will for you.'

'You may do what you like, Doctor,' he answered. 'See here!' he continued, handing a paper over to me, 'look at this!'

It was the *Echo* for the day, and the paragraph to which he pointed was devoted[3] to the case in question.

'The public,' it said, 'have lost a sensational treat[4] through the sudden death of the man Hope, who was suspected of the murder of Mr. Enoch Drebber and of Mr. Joseph Stangerson. The details of the case will probably be never known now, though we are informed upon good authority[5] that the crime was the result of an old-standing[6] and romantic feud[7], in which love and Mormonism bore a part[8]. It seems that both the victims belonged, in their younger days, to the Latter Day Saints, and Hope, the deceased prisoner, hails also from[9] Salt Lake City. If the case has had no other effect, it, at least, brings out[10] in the most striking manner the efficiency of our detective police force, and will serve as a lesson to all foreigners that they will do wisely[11] to settle their feuds[12] at home, and not to carry them on to British soil. It is an open secret[13] that the credit[14] of this smart capture belongs entirely to the well-known Scotland Yard officials, Messrs. Lestrade and Gregson. The man was apprehended, it appears, in the rooms of a certain Mr. Sherlock Holmes, who has himself, as an amateur, shown some talent in the detective line[15], and

1. dont j'avais déjà présumé l'existence
2. enchaînement logique sans interruption ni faille
3. consacré
4. a été privé d'un fabuleux plaisir
5. savons de bonne source
6. très ancienne
7. querelle
8. ont eu leur rôle
9. est également originaire de
10. elle met tout du moins en lumière
11. seraient avisés
12. de vider leurs querelles
13. secret de Polichinelle
14. mérite
15. en matière d'enquêtes

who, with such instructors, may hope in time to attain to some degree of their skill[1]. It is expected that a testimonial[2] of some sort will be presented[3] to the two officers as a fitting recognition[4] of their services.'

'Didn't I tell you so when we started?' cried Sherlock Holmes with a laugh. 'That's the result of all our Study in Scarlet: to get them a testimonial!'

'Never mind,' I answered, 'I have all the facts in my journal, and the public shall know them. In the meantime you must make yourself contented by[5] the consciousness of success, like the Roman miser[6]:

Populus me sibilat, at mihi plaudo
Ipse domi simul ac nummos contemplor in arca[7].

1. approcher de leur haut niveau de compétence
2. témoignage
3. rendu
4. en juste récompense
5. vous contenter
6. avare
7. Ils me sifflent, mais comme je m'applaudis lorsque chez moi je contemple mon argent, bien rangé dans mon coffre ! [*Satires* d'Horace]

La collection Yes you can!

Les faux débutants

Linwood Barclay *Broken Promise*

M. C. Beaton *Agatha Raisin and the Quiche of Death*

M. C. Beaton *Agatha Raisin and the Vicious Vet*

Harlan Coben *The Stranger*

Michael Connelly *The Black Box*

Michael Connelly *The Burning Room*

Michael Connelly *The Drop*

Michael Connelly *The Wrong Side of Goodbye*

Ken Follett *The Modigliani Scandal*

Mary Higgins Clark *A Cry in the Night*

Mary Higgins Clark *A Stranger is Watching*

Mary Higgins Clark *Loves Music, Loves to Dance*

Mary Higgins Clark *Where are the Children?*

Anthony Horowitz *The House of Silk*

George R. R. Martin *The Hedge Knight*

George R. R. Martin *The Sworn Sword*

George R. R. Martin *The Mystery Knight*

Ian Rankin *In a House of Lies*

Ian Rankin *Knots & Crosses*

Nicholas Sparks *Message in a Bottle*

Les intermédiaires

Harlan Coben *Caught*

Harlan Coben *Play Dead*

Harlan Coben *Stay Close*

Harlan Coben *Tell No One*

Harlan Coben *The Woods*

Ken Follett *Paper Money*

Anthony Horowitz *Moriarty*

P. D. James *A Mind to Murder*

P. D. James *Death Comes to Pemberley*

Douglas Kennedy *The Big Picture*

Stephen King *Finders Keepers*

Stephen King *The Green Mile*

John le Carré *A Most Wanted Man*

Les avancés

Paul Auster *Leviathan*

Paul Auster *Oracle Night*

Julian Barnes *The Sense of an Ending*

Michael Cunningham *By Nightfall*

Michael Cunningham *The Hours*

Helen Fielding *Bridget Jones's Diary*

Helen Fielding *Bridget Jones: The Edge of Reason*

Elizabeth George *A Great Deliverance*

Stephen King *Dolores Claiborne*

Stephen King *Misery*

Les classiques

Jane Austen *Pride and Prejudice*

Charlotte Brontë *Jane Eyre*

G. K. Chesterton *The Innocence of Father Brown*

Arthur Conan Doyle *A Study in Scarlet*

Arthur Conan Doyle *The Hound of the Baskervilles*

Francis Scott Fitzgerald *Tender is the Night*

Francis Scott Fitzgerald *The Great Gatsby*

Washington Irving, Arthur Conan Doyle, Edgar Allan Poe *The Legend of Sleepy Hollow and Other Scary Stories*

George Orwell *Animal Farm*

George Orwell *1984*

Edgar Allan Poe *The Fall of the House of Usher and Other Stories*

Mary Shelley *Frankenstein*

Bram Stoker *Dracula*

Edith Wharton *The Age of Innocence*

Oscar Wilde *The Importance of Being Earnest*

Oscar Wilde *The Picture of Dorian Gray*

Virginia Woolf *To the Lighthouse*

PAPIER À BASE DE FIBRES CERTIFIÉES

HARRAP s'engage pour l'environnement en réduisant l'empreinte carbone de ses livres. Celle de cet exemplaire est de :
600 g éq. CO_2
Rendez-vous sur www.larousse-durable.fr

Imprimé en Italie par Grafica Veneta
Dépôt légal : mai 2021
327734-02/ 11050778 - mai 2022